Final Deception

FINAL DECEPTION

Final Deception

A Whidbey Island Mystery

Dan Pedersen

Mysteries by the Author
Available from Whidbey Island bookstores and Amazon.com

Final Deception: *A Whidbey Island Mystery (Book 1)*
Final Passage: *Mystery on the Alaska Ferry (Book 2)*
Final Escape: *Mystery in the Idaho Sawtooths (Book 3)*
Final Justice: *Mystery on Whidbey Island (Book 4)*
Final Pursuit: *Mystery in the Adirondacks (Book 5)*
Final Impulse: *Mystery on Whidbey Island*

Other Titles by the Author:
Wild Whidbey: *The Nature of Island Life*
Whidbey Island's Special Places (not sold by Amazon)
Louis and Fanny: *15 Years on the Alaska Frontier*
Outdoorsy Male: *Short Stories and Essays*

Dedication

For Candace, JoAnn, Chris, Dave and Regina.

Contents

FINAL DECEPTION

Acknowledgments

In 2013, while searching online for an old friend, I discovered her obituary. She was a fellow journalist and confidant with whom I once shared many adventures and soul-searching talks. She died alone in another state before her time, and I waited too long to look for her.

She left a thin trail but I located her last known friend who explained she had become a recluse and withdrawn from her family and nearly all who once knew her, including at times him.

Honoring her last wish, this friend brought her ashes home to Washington and convened a small gathering of her former newspaper colleagues on the shores of Puget Sound. We who loved her long ago shared our sadness as we pieced together a life filled with secrets. We reached for words – difficult, demanding, imperfect, unforgettable, gifted, unlucky in love.

She was the inspiration for *Final Deception,* my exploration of friendship, fidelity and aging, and the circumstances that cause us to turn away from the world. The story honors the qualities I most admired in her and other good friends in the fictional character Bella Morelli. I built the story around the conflict that divides the Whidbey Island community, the controversy over Navy jet noise.

The story draws from personal experiences and friendships, but most heavily from 30 years of island life. Readers who know the area will recognize many of the settings. The story is entirely fiction. None of the characters or events are real.

I owe special thanks to those friends who shared their perspective as private pilots and military pilots, those who helped me discover the joys of nature, and all who shaped this manuscript. That includes Paul and Brigid, Bill, Don, Craig and Joy, Karen, Janis and Pat.

FINAL DECEPTION

Chapter 1

Four Seconds

In the blackness, Bella Morelli pitched face forward in an ungainly dive, wind roaring in her ears. The four seconds took forever and she had two last thoughts – surprise and dread. She hit the water all wrong like a breaching whale, lungs first, a horrible impact, and that was the last she felt.

*

Deception Pass Bridge connects Washington's Fidalgo and Whidbey Islands across a deep chasm. It is 180 feet from the bridge deck to the water, depending on tide. From there it's 130 more in icy darkness to the bottom.

A young person in peak condition, hitting the water feet first in perfect form, can survive if they miss the rocks and regain the surface before drowning or hypothermia. A 67-year-old cannot. Whirlpools and eddies reach out to clutch and pull them down.

Most who survive the impact drown anyway, gruesomely injured. Typical damage is smashed spines and crushed internal organs, brain injury and burst blood vessels from the pressure difference. Fractured ribs from crushed rib cages penetrate the lungs and liver.

Currents here can reach 8 knots. Bodies found days or weeks later float on the outgoing tide as far as Dead Man's Bay on San Juan Island, just south of the headland at Lime Kiln State Park, one of the world's preeminent locations to watch whales from shore.

If they're found at all.

Chapter 2

Last Words

Bridge Claims Another Life

Sheriff's deputies recovered the body Tuesday of Isabella Morelli, 67, of Coupeville, Washington. She was found by a tour boat east of Deception Pass Bridge on Whidbey Island. A spokesman said her injuries were consistent with a fall from the bridge, and the death is being investigated as a suicide. Ms. Morelli had been a journalist for several newspapers including most notably *The Washington Post*. She was known for her penetrating stories about the men and women of the military, especially those who had served in combat and suffered psychological injuries.

*

Brad Haraldsen wiped a tear from his cheek and stared at the words on his screen. Suicide?

That wasn't Bella.

From the living room of his foothills ranch, he'd been watching the first rays of daybreak flood the razor-backed peaks of Idaho's Sawtooth Mountains. How he loved the morning. Pockets of snow still clung to the heights around Stanley, and the valley floor was a carpet of purple Camas flowers.

But this morning his heart ached. Over the years he had wondered where Bella was, what she was doing and whether she was happy. It comforted him knowing she was out there – somewhere. This morning, in a moment of curiosity, he'd Googled her name.

He'd been writing an uplifting column for his weekly piece on National Public Radio. Now suddenly, he could not work.

Had he missed a call for help?

After a silence of decades, Bella had crossed through his life two weeks ago with a cryptic, do-not-reply email.

Got myself in deep. Probably nothing, but if anything happens, find my computer. Don't reply to this email.

The email hadn't mentioned where she was. What was she doing 3,000 miles from home, dead, under a bridge?

Last he'd known, she lived in a Georgetown condominium in Washington, D.C., surrounded by art, and walked miles every day in the nation's capital. She'd always said there were too many automobiles in the world and a car was more trouble than it was worth. She thrived on culture and politics, and public transportation.

He had let the email pass, mindful that the screwed-up timing of their lives made anything more moot. Maybe there would come a time to try again. He wasn't sure. It depended on the woman in the next room, or more truthfully, on him.

He could just hear Irene's rhythmic snoring from the bedroom. Beautiful Irene. She would sleep hours longer, then wander the house in her robe till noon. This was his time to think, and already he knew what he must do.

In the distance, the Salmon River shimmered as it wound past the cluster of log buildings that was old Stanley. He loved the River of No Return, the ribbon of water that meandered through this highland basin. In sleepy Stanley it gathered speed as it began a tortured course through the state's uninhabitable middle to the Snake on the other side, and the huge Columbia beyond that, draining the Northwest all the way to the Pacific.

Something had taken Bella past her own point of no return. She had never backed down from a fight, never been at a loss for words. Now she could no longer speak for herself. If she'd been silenced, someone else must stand up for her and Brad knew it could only be him.

This would be complicated. He and Bella had never told anyone their secret. Investigating her death would add to the strain on a marriage already at the breaking point.

Stepping inside, he listened for the last gurgle and beep of the coffeemaker as it finished its work. He poured his first cup, crossed the room to his den off the kitchen, and sat down, letting the cup warm his hands as he stared at the computer.

*

Brad had never stopped thinking of Bella. A lifetime ago he had held onto hope much too long for a future with her. Only when she married a Syrian bureaucrat had Brad found a partner of his own, Irene.

Neither marriage had been a storybook romance. Brad's started well but he and Irene now lived together essentially as roommates, increasingly apart emotionally. They had married in their late 30s and never had children, but filled the early years of their marriage with dogs, horses and friends. It was one adventure after another, often cooked up by Irene and her best friend Amy, wife of Brad's college roommate, Stu Wood.

Stu and Amy lived in Rigby and flew often to Stanley in Stu's airplane for weekends with Brad and Irene. The two women loved to picnic in the worst way, as Brad put it. He smiled, remembering the time Amy and Irene led their husbands on a backcountry ride in the hills behind the tiny, mountain community of Featherville on the South Fork Boise.

"It's just the most beautiful, pristine country, and we can go places with the horses that nobody ever sees," Irene promised. "Stu can catch a few trout and you can take pictures." So they set out for the hinterlands behind Al Anderson Reservoir on gravel roads in Irene's

King Cab Super Duty, pulling a four-horse trailer loaded with all their tack.

A day of riding mountain trails brought them to a good clearing on a sandbar by an icy, waist-high creek, where they pitched tents and roasted bratwurst, and laid on their backs and gazed at the Milky Way, and talked about the friendship they hoped would never end.

"Thank god for these horses," Amy said. "We'd never be here if it weren't for them, but I gotta say my butt is killing me."

Irene rummaged in her pack and produced a jar of Doc's Saddle Sore Ointment. "Put this in your pocket and take a little walk out back, and slather it where you need to. You'll feel better in the morning," she assured Amy. And they all turned in for a hard night's sleep.

The next thing Irene felt was a hand shaking her shoulder.

"The horses are gone," Amy said. "And something's moving in the bushes."

"Mountain lion," Irene declared, sitting bolt upright. "That's why the horses took off. I didn't tether them because I was sure they'd graze and stay with us at the campsite. Let's get some wood on the fire and build it up to keep the cat away."

That was the end of sleep. The foursome spent the next few hours feeding the fire and staring into the shadows as the invisible shape circled their campsite, intentions unknown, just out of view. By daybreak, incoherent and groggy, the campers concluded the lion was gone. Now to locate the horses.

Irene put some sugar cubes in her pocket, forded the creek and picked up the trail of hoof prints on the far bank, following it two miles downstream and returning to camp in late morning with all four.

"A Basque sheep herder caught and tethered them to his wagon," she said. "Or I might have been gone longer."

Hours behind schedule, they began the all-day ride back to Featherville and a night drive back to the ranch in Stanley, where they piled into real beds at 3 a.m.

"Wasn't that just the best time!" Irene asked Brad at 11:00 the next morning as they sat comatose over toast and eggs.

"Yes, if you mean losing the horses and being held hostage all night by a mountain lion."

It was that adventurous spirit, and Irene's love of books and entertaining, that had attracted him to her in the first place. Stylish, tall and brunette, she could captivate any visitor. They skied at Sun Valley and entertained often in their home with good wine and great meals, and conversation to suit.

The good times with Stu and Amy ended five years ago when Amy died in a one-car accident on her way to pick up Irene for a day together. Since then Brad saw little of Stu anymore, and Irene drifted deeper into her wine, mostly withdrawing from him emotionally, busying herself with mindless tasks.

Was it grief? Brad wondered. Survivor's guilt – *Why wasn't I in that car with her?* Aging is complicated, Brad knew, the losses and depression, and all the questions time raises about the difference one's life makes. He was struggling with enough depression and guilt of his own after failing to help his brother.

When you've watched someone close die, as Brad did with his brother, every additional day you get seems an undeserved gift. Brad did not take life for granted. A day starts fresh and unlimited. How it ends, well, that is the question. The possibilities of the morning only make the ache of unfulfilled dreams worse. Brad's marriage was suffocating and he worried he was the reason. Irene deserved better than he was giving.

Any more, Brad simply relished the contemplative quiet of the morning. Nothing stopped him from rising before dawn to watch the valley awaken.

Bella would not see this dawn. Brad couldn't change that but he could find out why. He still had the fragile gift of life, and still had words to write.

As soon as Irene was up, he'd tell her what he must do.

Chapter 3

Baby Birds

Bella had been increasingly sure of what she must do, as well. Her decision was months in the making, the culmination of many separate moments that put her on the path that led to the bridge that ended finally in the words Brad was reading on his screen.

None of those moments stood apart especially – just snapshots of everyday life, such as the afternoon months earlier in her back yard in Admiral's Cove. She had been lost in thought when . . .

"Is that for your hummingbirds?" the little voice asked, startling her. Surrounded by hedges of Nootka Rose, salal and huckleberry, Bella thought she was quite alone as she hung her hummingbird feeder in her brushy yard.

But in a thin spot in the hedge, where a little-used path led by a back way to homes down the road, she picked out a face staring straight at her – a boy, about five, framed by the brush. Blonde and blue-eyed, he had bangs clear down to the top of his nose. He wore a red-checked flannel shirt, tucked neatly into a pair of stiff, new blue jeans.

What touched Bella's heart was the tilt of his head and his parted lips, as if he were thinking hard.

"My name is Bella," she called to him. "What's your name?"

"Billy," he said. "Billy Lindstrom." And then he added, "We have baby birds."

"You do?"

"Um, um . . . in a box my dad made."

"Your dad must be a very nice man."

"He carries a gun but would never hurt the birds. Do you want to see our birds?"

"Yes," Bella said. "Will you show me?"

The boy took Bella's hand and led her through the hedge, along a marshy shore of cattails and drainage channels, to the back yard of a newer, single-story home.

"Is your dad in the Navy?" Bella asked.

"No he's a deputy sheriff."

In the back yard of Billy's home, a pair of forked-tail birds swooped gracefully back-and-forth across the yard and nearby marsh, in turn hovering briefly at the opening of a box atop a post before climbing into the air again and resuming their hunt. Several little heads reached out of the box, cheeping loudly.

"Those are Violet-green Swallows," Bella said. "Very special birds."

"I know," Billy said. "I like them."

"I do, too," Bella said. "Did you see the beautiful male, standing guard atop the box?"

In the distance, a low roar grew louder and then rose to a shriek as a US Navy jet passed a few hundred feet overhead, gear and flaps down, so low they could see the crew in the cockpit. Bella and Billy covered their ears. Even as the first jet dipped below the nearby trees, Bella could see a second in the distance, circling to follow it on the same approach.

"It's going to be noisy now for a while," Bella said.

"I know," Billy replied. "It hurts my ears."

"You should get inside and I'm going to run back and put my dog Ida in the house where it's quieter," Bella said. We'll talk about birds some more soon."

Chapter 4

The Forest

Bella gazed up at the backlit canopy of green and felt dizzy. She was thinking about the trees. They had stood in this place for generations – through fire and saws, freak winds, winter snows and summer droughts, and the incremental pounding of millions of human feet.

Loggers in the 1800s, harvesting the island's seemingly inexhaustible old growth, left a few here that were too stunted or inaccessible to be worth their trouble. Now they were monarchs, relics of time prized for all they had silently witnessed.

This short walk in the forest was Bella's private secret, hers and Ida's. It was good to explore with a dog, she thought, because the dog moved in another dimension. The dog's nose found details otherwise missed – coyote scat on a decomposing log, the near presence of a doe with fawns, the memory of last night's raccoon.

The Wilbert Trail was where Bella often came to reflect in the cool freshness and clarity of the woods. It saddened her that places like this were embattled everywhere by the forces of "progress." An ecologist she'd interviewed pointed out that the forest has few defenders in the push to harvest more lumber, build more houses, generate property tax revenue, lay asphalt and build burger joints and box stores.

For Bella, discovering the forest was the great epiphany of part two of her life. The forest was alien to most people's reality, she knew, but it was where she now felt most whole and at peace. How could one feel otherwise, she wondered, as she walked past an ancient cedar in an ocean of sword ferns as high as her head?

How different this was from the world of leaf blowers, night clubs, cheap Chinese goods, guns, plastic, violent sports, fireworks, chainsaws, TV and smart phones, jet planes, lawns and weed-killers.

The forest was random, uncontrolled, perfect and complete. A tree fell here, upturning its root ball and exposing mineral earth there. Seeds fell to the clearing and took hold. Dead trees – snags – stood among the living, and woodpeckers drilled cavities that became homes for more creatures.

In fact dead wood was the life force of this place. Fallen trees decomposed, first as nurse logs for other trees, later as organic mulch to enrich the forest floor. With no help from man, the centuries designed a complex-canopied, mixed-species forest of conifers and broadleafs, a perfect system. This one had Douglas Fir and Western Hemlock, Western Red Cedar, Red Alder, Western White Pine, Sitka Spruce and Big Leaf Maple. And it sustained a magnificent ecosystem of owls and woodpeckers, nuthatches and chickadees, raccoons, squirrels, snakes, salamanders, frogs and countless other species.

More and more Bella preferred solitude and the company of these trees and the forest's creatures to her fellow humans. Was that wrong?

Perhaps it reflected the inevitable decline of age. If so she would own it. Society placed a high value on extroverts, those who chitchatted and fit in, pleased others and came to life in crowds. More and more, Bella shunned the crowds and small talk, and felt her introversion was a gift. Age amplified her ability to think and feel deeply, to notice and care about details and connections, to go against the crowd.

The thinking she'd done here was the clearest and best of her life. And to be alone at times was exquisitely peaceful. Cancer had taught her not to fear the silence but to cherish it, to embrace reflection, the comfort of her own thoughts.

A shaft of sunlight pierced the trees and illuminated the floor of a wetland pool. Ida stopped to lap up the cool, clear water. It seeped from the uplands and emerged here on the surface in trickling creeks and crystal clear ponds surrounded by deer ferns. Those uplands, the Trillium Forest, had been butchered in a clear cut some years ago, then saved from development by an outpouring of community fundraising. It would be decades – centuries – before they approached in beauty this Classic U remnant, but their salvation represented the hope of the future.

The trail meandered deeper into the wetland. Here, Bella knew she walked on a floating mat of forest duff two feet deep, made perfect over centuries, suspended by the massive living roots of the surrounding trees. She could feel it – jump up and down and feel the ground bounce.

She met hikers hurrying to reach the end. And then what? She wondered if they gained anything, the experience over. Did they even know where they were, what miracles lay beneath their feet and all around?

The question that bedeviled her was how to convey this to readers, to open their eyes to the intrinsic value of places like this. She knew this must be part of the larger story she was writing.

For some, she realized, the eye opening began with something as small as a hummingbird feeder. Introduced to hummingbirds, they might wonder for the first time about a creature that accepted their charity yet migrated thousands of miles, beyond human control. Or perhaps Bald Eagles. Everyone loved the national symbol, maybe only because it was unmistakable and large, and violent.

Human values were endlessly in conflict, she recognized, and on the island the competing values often collided. The island attracted some because they already loved nature and sought a life closer to it. Others made the discovery in little degrees over time, came to an entirely different way of thinking than they brought with them from somewhere else.

And a few never changed. They pursued the only values they knew, material gain and consumption.

Her thoughts returned to a favorite Bible verse, Mark 8:36. "For what does it profit a man if he shall gain the whole world, and lose his own soul?"

She wished more people of faith took that to heart.

Chapter 5

Faith

More and more, Bella wondered whether faith made any difference at all in the collision of material and spiritual values. Was faith the solution to human differences or just a crutch both sides used to justify them?

The central value of all faiths is love, she believed, yet so often people of faith build walls and deny the common humanity of others, and exploit the earth, and even take infidels' lives in a twisted interpretation of religious duty. It is the story of human history.

During the months of chemotherapy and reentry into what Bella now saw as part two of her life, she'd had time to think about this. She was raised a Catholic and looked to her faith for strength.

Faith had always been her moral compass. During her university years it compelled her to protest the Vietnam War and march for civil rights. She would do it again. It also instilled in her a deep sense of guilt and unworthiness, and guided her to a confusing approach to dating and sex. This she might not do again.

But those years were easy compared to these. As an older woman, her new perspective on faith challenged every assumption she held about her place in the world. The forces of resistance were overwhelming.

With no children or close friends to support her during the fight with cancer, Bella had leaned on her parish priest, Father William

Benedict, and he had devoted himself to her. She could not imagine surviving without his lifeline. But now as she found renewed energy to participate in life, she saw other sides of Benedict that disturbed her – the man's all-too-human frailties and complexities. She saw flashes of ego, temper and impatience, an odd remoteness, and a preoccupation with the business of the church. More ominous was the touching. Children are naturally affectionate – hugging and touching one another – but did an adult priest's physicality cross a line?

Benedict's obsession with appearances troubled her. He ran the lawn sprinklers on a timer every morning, rain or shine, and hired a garden service to green-up the church's grounds with chemical fertilizers and weed killers. Hispanics with leaf blowers ran the noisy machines for hours as they blew all the leaves and dust out of the gutters and sidewalks, down the street toward the Mormon church, which had its own Hispanics blowing them back. It all seemed curiously ironic because he was Hispanic, too. He courted real estate developers, car dealers and CEOs of island institutions as church investors and benefactors.

Benedict had taken over a dying parish and revitalized it. The town celebrated him for that. But in the process he had forged alliances with people of means, big givers, who often were those with the heaviest footprints on earth. Some had even written letters to the editor complaining of the waste of public resources on parks and open space nobody needs, that generate nothing in revenue for the county.

Bella found more sympathetic company when she visited those open spaces than when she went to church. What she noticed was a spiritual quality in the people she met outdoors. She could feel their reverence for nature and wildlife –for the miracle of life itself. Walkers by and large were sensitive, thoughtful people, aware of nature's connections and their place in the web of it all – seeking balance for both mental and physical health.

Increasingly, Bella was drawn toward a Franciscan outlook, embracing a life of simplicity and respect for all living things, shunning needless consumption. She liked the new Pope Francis.

An Audubon friend steered her to read Rachel Carson, in whom she found a sister of sorts. Carson had died at age 56 of breast cancer after writing *Silent Spring* about American's chemical companies. The big chemical companies had instilled in the postwar generation the tragic idea that chemical pesticides were the keys to better living. Society had paid a price for that and was still paying it. Was it the source of her own cancer? She'd never know.

Bella could no longer kill a spider. That was the proof of her transformation. Simplicity and humility were contrary to the values of many, especially in this setting with stunning marine views, and personal wealth and material possessions.

Her husband Majed, from her first life, had been a mistake born of her own desperation. She was a different person then and had been taken in by his urbane taste, handsome good looks, love of art and reading, his passion for politics and current affairs, and his belief in a supreme being, be it God or Allah as he called him. The difference in names seemed unimportant at the time.

Where Majed was now, she had no idea. She hoped her abrupt move to the far coast and a rental house owned in someone else's name had left no trail for him to follow. But in this world of online public records it is hard to erase all traces. She looked over her shoulder.

By degrees she had drifted to a place in her own mind that set her apart from most people and the life she'd once known. She lived simply, abhorred noise, cherished peace, loved nature. She was especially distressed by the US Navy's increasing grip on the island's soul and its assault on all she held dear.

She felt some safety from Majed and island reactionaries in the protection of Benedict and the cop next door, Shane Lindstrom. But were they befriending her or watching her?

She was not sure.

Chapter 6

Hiding Out

Elbows on his desk, Brad propped his head in his hands. A tear rolled down his cheek. Bella had dropped out of sight years ago and he had no idea why.

An urban Easterner, she had ended her days in the rural West, on an island in Puget Sound. It did not fit. What puzzled him was that whatever had brought her there, and whatever she had gotten into, it was bigger and more dangerous than all the other battles she'd ever fought.

People have their private reasons for disappearing, he knew. They are running from childhood pain, failed relationships, death, their personal demons. A friend once confessed to him, "I'm just hiding out. It's why I work nights and sleep during the day."

In hindsight Brad wondered if he could have changed what happened. In 1975, when his older brother Jim reached out for help, Brad misjudged the depth of Jim's crisis.

Jim had returned from Vietnam unable to sleep, to think, to have a girlfriend or to work. Brad tried to help him re-enter but knew there was something Jim wasn't sharing. "For god's sake," Brad told Jim, "if you don't talk about it you'll never be able to put it behind you."

"And if I do, you'll never speak to me again," Jim said. "I should never have come back from that war."

"Nothing could be that bad."

Jim stared at him for a minute, then spoke in a hoarse whisper, "We burned people alive. I didn't stop it and now I can't shut out the screams, the smell of children burning. We burned families in their grass huts. For what?"

Brad thought Jim would pull himself together in time, pick up his life. He was in and out of veterans' hospitals and support groups, but preferred the company of his drug buddies. Brad took him fishing and hiking, sat up with him at night during the bad dreams, and took him away camping on the 4th of July. Jim had already had a lifetime's worth of bombs bursting in air.

In 1977, just as Brad's journalism career was taking hold amid the pristine beauty of Idaho, Jim drove his car into a tree at 100 miles per hour. He hadn't outrun his pain. He left a note to Brad in his apartment. "Have a good life, little bro. Tell the truth."

To fight Brad's own pain, he wrote his own prescription – found his niche telling positive stories of hope and inspiration. He sought, and found, Idaho neighbors whose lives embodied quiet strength and contribution, who lifted up others and made their communities a better place.

Newspapers affectionately named him *Idaho's Storyteller* and he gained a coveted, weekly segment on National Public Radio's Morning Edition. He wondered if Bella listened. He never saw himself as an investigative journalist or fighter like Bella – didn't have the stomach for it – just wanted to give people something positive in their lives.

In his circle Bella was the courageous one. She had been his first love. He knew with the clarity of hindsight you only get one of those.

If Bella had chosen Deception Pass Bridge for her final act, it seemed a crushing defeat and almost a pointed message to him. The bridge and its surrounding park had been a getaway of theirs throughout college, when he and Bella studied journalism together at the University of Washington. He had brought Bella here several times at night – always platonically – after an evening at some college pub, to talk and share a favorite beach from his childhood. But the bridge's reputation for suicides was well known even then, half a century ago.

While the bridge's reputation did not prove Bella jumped, the setting implied it. Age brings depression, a view of the end, sadness and guilt, Brad knew.

Had something weighed so heavily on Bella that this was her only escape? She'd always made impossibly high demands on herself, yet didn't seem the type to surrender to sadness. But then, he'd barely heard a word from her in 30 years.

Brad believed in every life there is a defining script – a sense of self through which we filter and interpret everything, and from which we cannot deviate. We might see ourselves as the perpetual victim, survivor, martyr or avenger. This, combined with some turning point, picks our battles for us and determines whether we win or lose. Bella was a fighter.

Something had put Bella on the bridge – something she saw or heard, a chance remark to the wrong person, a quarrel or question too many, someone she met, or knew, or loved, or a pain so great she could fight no more.

People choose who they want to be, Brad believed. This choice becomes a self-fulfilling prophecy. Bella was who she was for a reason, and this reason had led her to the bridge, either by her own decision or someone else's.

Journalism turns some people into cynics and fighters. It made Brad more optimistic and hopeful. He attributed the optimism to a happy childhood and good genes, and parents who believed life got better with each passing year. It was Brad's second-grade teacher who set him on this path. She made her classroom a make-believe village called Happyville, and every citizen published his own version of its happenings in his own newspaper, *The Happyville News*.

When Brad's parents saw the earliest spark of an interest in writing, they bought him a child's printing press, and the presses had not stopped rolling since.

Investigating is the nature of a journalist's job, talking with people, asking questions, noticing details, connecting the dots. He loved it with every fiber of his being and remembered how excited he and Bella, and Stu, had been every day of their university careers.

Every life is a story. People and their stories fascinated Brad, and sometimes made him sad as was the case with his friend, Stu.

His best friend had a very different script for his life – saw himself as the perpetual victim and underdog who struggled under a dark cloud and never got a break. Brad wished he could change that. Stu did not share Brad's faith in people and really preferred the solitude of nature and the outdoors. Even when things went well in his life, Stu rarely recognized it. Brad knew chronic depression ran in Stu's family. He managed surprisingly well but had little positive to say of his childhood and family.

Brad wondered if Bella had any conscious awareness of the turning point in her life, the moment that set her course. Whatever it was, it had been far from Brad's thoughts five decades ago in college. Back then he saw Bella as a young woman full of dreams, often secretive, at times flirty, always brilliant, ever hungry to find the truth.

Chapter 7

Hate

Traitors like Isabella Morelli hate our country, hate our Navy and hate Whidbey Island. She is not one of us and never will be. Why does she hide she is married to a Muslim?

The sooner this evil woman goes, the better.

The vitriol astounded Brad. He knew Bella had married a Muslim but this was beyond imagination. He made a steeple of his fingers as he stared, online, at the letters page of the island news. After finding the death notice he was trying to make sense of Bella's life of recent years. Was this really his beautiful friend of a lifetime ago – despised and rejected in her own community?

The terrorists hate our freedoms and the brave men who defend them, the letter declared. *I want my country back! Socialist foreigners and Muslims have no right to tell us what to think. They are cancers in our community.*

Chapter 8

Love

Decades ago Brad had almost cracked the mystery of Bella. She had taken a road trip with him, taken a risk. Brad registered them in a Tennessee motel as Mr. and Mrs. Brad Haraldsen.

They hadn't discussed the sleeping arrangement – it just happened. They were two unmarried 25-year-olds traveling in the South in 1972. Gatlinburg was a honeymoon destination and the couple's eyes glistened with new love. Even in civilian attire, Brad carried himself with military bearing. That and his clean-cut, neatly trimmed hair were assets in the South where patriotism ran high.

As it was, the clerk didn't question their marital status – gave them a room by the pool in the nearly vacant auto court.

A heavy sky threatened afternoon lightning. Brad and Bella swam anyway and washed the miles from the road. Then, five years into their friendship, they made love for the first time as comfortably as if it were every day.

The lovemaking was slow and satisfying, their private secret as the storm rumbled through the lush hills beyond the thick curtains. Afterwards, they lay in each other's arms. Bella smiled and Brad felt her caution about him wash away.

A lifetime later, sitting on his mountain in Stanley, Idaho, Brad still teared up at the memory, as vivid now as it had ever been. That time, that place to which they had never returned, was the happiest of his life. Brad's eyes stung and he closed them to see it all again. He remembered every detail of that motel, that room, the long journey that led there.

He was glad he had driven cross-country to see Bella. With her shoulder length, raven hair and hazel eyes, Isabella had been a seductive mystery throughout their university years. Brad saw her as deeply private and circumspect – a second-generation, only child of Italian immigrants who sacrificed and denied their own comforts so she could have opportunities they never did.

Traditional and Catholic, she was also a product of the confused 60s who went bra-less on principle, then folded her arms across her chest in modesty. With an unrelenting work ethic and deep sense of inadequacy, she was hard to get to know, slow to confide in others.

Brad, by contrast, concealed nothing but his politics, which were anti-war, and his atheism, which he politely never imposed. He was clean-cut and fit from military service, an all-American superimposed on something harder to define.

Brad, Bella and Stu were the three stars of campus journalism at the University of Washington in the 1960s, attending classes in the daytime, writing stories for *The Daily* in the afternoon, then going home in the evening to debate the day's issues over dinner at the residence hall.

They were the newspaper's A-team for anti-war protests, Students for a Democratic Society, The Weather Underground and the embattled university administration, struggling to keep order.

Looking back now Brad could laugh, but in school Bella had tied him and Stu in knots. He still marveled at her sheer drive, always one step ahead.

He hadn't forgotten the time he brought the editor a scoop about a radical group's plans to lead a peace march across the interstate freeway bridge through Seattle and close it to traffic.

"This is outstanding!" the editor congratulated him. "If it were any other day I'd banner it all over page 1, but all I can give you on the front tomorrow is a short tease and a jump inside."

He added, "I have to bump Stu inside, too." The editor gave page 1 to Bella. She had spent two hours with Bobby Kennedy the previous afternoon and he bared his soul about his brother and Lyndon Johnson. It was riveting.

"I had a feeling Bella could draw him out and she did," the editor said.

She was an undeniable force. With her fierce work ethic and captivating, breathless voice, she nearly always won her subject's trust and landed the big interview.

Brad, too, was well aware of that voice and smitten with the mysterious woman behind it. He was afraid if he said too much about that, too soon in their senior year, he'd frighten her off. He sensed Stu was weighing the same calculation.

"Don't you think she's hot?" Stu asked one afternoon as he and Brad tossed a Frisbee on the commons lawn.

"Well yeah," Brad said, "but she's more than that. She's complex and deep. She's balancing a lot of conflict and family expectations, real or imagined. She isn't easy to get to know."

"That's where I disagree," Stu said. "She just wants people to think she's complex. I think she's aching for someone to show some interest, take her dancing and help her lighten up and have fun. I'll bet she's never gone camping, fishing, boating or skiing."

"Probably not," Brad agreed. "But I think that would bomb."

As graduation loomed, Brad worried that a wrong move would poison the collegial chemistry and drive her away before they even finished school. With the military waiting for him, he fumbled his chances. He was too cautious. Stu stepped in and asked Bella out, and she said yes.

It devastated Brad – betrayed by his best friend. Even worse, it tortured Brad that Bella might secretly have wanted Stu all along. Would the most miserable months of Brad's life now be the happiest of Stu and Bella's?

Stu and Bella dated only a few months, till Brad was away in military training. Brad could only guess how serious it was or what they had shared. Almost as suddenly as Stu started seeing her, he broke it off. By then, the damage to Brad's chances was done and Bella was grieving. She wrote Brad that she had cut off all her hair.

Now, three years later, Brad felt his time had come again, probably for the last time.

Bella had taken an internship at *The Washington Post*, as far as she could get from both Brad and Stu. Brad was stationed in the tumbleweed country of southern Idaho in the Air Force, quietly riding out a four-year enlistment. First-term airmen rarely went to war. Army draftees almost always did.

He had called and written Bella for months, flirted on the phone as much as he could. Though he and Stu saw each other often, he never mentioned that to Bella. He appealed to her sympathies for an unwilling soldier, victim of an unjust system that made a mockery of his intelligence.

"The Air Force mops floors," he told Bella. "And it marches. That's what all the college grads do with our university educations. Maybe it's the military's way of getting back at us for our independent thinking. We spend all our spare time on chicken shit."

"I thought you worked in base personnel, writing bad conduct discharges," Bella interjected.

"I do, but the Air Force always finds time for the other."

"I feel for you," she said. "You're throwing away four years polishing floors while I write for the *Post* and Stu weasels out on a medical deferment."

"I'm crossing off the days," Brad said. "It'll be over soon. Idaho beats Vietnam and I love my off-duty hours at the little *Tumbleweed Times* in town. Small-town journalism is the most fun I ever had."

Then he took a risk.

"Let's get away on a road trip," he suggested. "I've earned some leave. I'll drive east, pick you up, and we'll see some new country for a few days."

"I'd like that – like to see you," she said. "As for the road trip, we'll talk about that when you get here. I won't say yes or no. From what I've told my Mother, she thinks you're a nice boy, but she would not approve of this. Nor would my faith."

She had been a mystery then – tantalizingly close to revealing herself. Discovering her secrets now would be harder than ever.

Chapter 9

Crockett Lake

Curled on a plush dog bed with her nose tucked under her tail, Idaho watched with one eye as Bella reached for her walking shoes.

The golden retriever stirred, lifted her head and tilted it far back.

"Rooooooooooooooh," she sang.

"I'm hurrying," Bella replied. "You're in fine voice."

Daybreak was Bella's favorite hour to walk the shore at Keystone Spit and Crockett Lake, minutes from her cottage. The breeze was brisk off Admiralty Inlet, and the Olympic Mountains still wore their winter coat of snow. The early morning world was at peace, silent and still. It was a good time to think and reflect, especially pleasant because at this hour few cars traveled the highway to the ferry terminal.

More important, Navy EA-18 Growler jets rarely performed touch-and-go landings this early at the nearby outlying practice field, though the same could not be said about nighttime. The jets had kept Bella awake till midnight the previous evening as they descended onto the short practice field and then roared back into the blackness trailing a tongue of fire, simulating nighttime landings on the deck of an aircraft carrier.

Heading out the door, Bella set a brisk pace to the end of the block, eager to reach the first drainage canals of the marsh. Where the lawns and tidy yards ended, Bella knew she would enter the world of nature. What she did not know was that today she'd have company.

There, bathed in the golden, low-angle light of the early morning stood a slim, middle-aged couple in matching, olive drab shirts with binoculars and a camera. The man was training a 400mm zoom lens on a narrow ditch in the cattails.

"Just watching a Great-blue Heron," he announced to Bella in a hushed voice before she could even ask. "I'm waiting for it to spear some breakfast."

Birders are an odd lot, Bella thought, mindful she had become one as well. They obsess about details, tiny differences that mere mortals overlook. More importantly, they notice the connections in nature – migration patterns, habitat health, the food chain, predators, interspecies relationships.

Bella stood reverently with the couple and watched the dinosaur-like creature creep ahead in knee-deep water, raising first one bony leg and then the other with supreme self-control. The angular bird stared intently at the water, its long bill poised to strike the next fish or amphibian that swam into view.

In the distance, a flock of geese honked as they passed over the marsh, and Idaho turned to watch. Bella let the sights and sounds soak in. "It's nice, isn't it, girl?" she spoke soothingly in a breathless whisper.

"You sure have a nice dog there," the man remarked. "She's calm and respectful of the birds. Do you walk here often?"

"Every morning," Bella replied. "I can't get enough of the fresh air and birds after years on the East Coast with nothing but transit buses, diesel fumes, crowds, litter and panhandlers."

She could have added she would never have made this move if Majed's threats and her own cancer had not challenged every assumption of her life. Friends admonished her, "Focus totally on getting well. Surround yourself with peace and beauty and make each day count."

"I had cancer," Bella suddenly volunteered, surprising herself. "This place and this walk are my second life, something I do entirely for myself."

"That's pretty much why we do it, too," the man said, taking his eye off the heron and offering his hand to Bella. "My name is Bill and this is my wife, Winkie."

"The first Winkie I've ever met in my life," Bella laughed as she then introduced herself.

"The story is that I winked at the nurse after she delivered me," Winkie explained. "But tell me, you're a long way from the East Coast. How did that happen?"

Bella liked these people and felt safe with them, and laid it all out. When she got the breast cancer diagnosis, doctors warned her she could fight it for a while with chemotherapy but probably wouldn't win. She decided right then to make her last stand in a quiet place away from stress and pressure.

Boston friends had spoken wistfully of an idyllic cabin in the San Juan Islands of Washington, but to Bella that seemed too remote. Whidbey offered much the same beauty, along with access to the Seattle Cancer Care Alliance, and local hospitals and services she would likely need along the way.

"I had a boyfriend long ago who grew up on Whidbey," she said. "He would never believe I ended up here, because this was the life he always romanticized and wanted for me – for us – but I wanted something else. I understand what he meant now. Getting a dog never crossed my mind either in five decades of city life, but here it makes sense. Ida is my constant companion, my security system and my guide to all the best details of nature."

As Bella talked, Bill steered her eye with a nod toward a Northern Harrier as it swooped, hovered and reversed direction over the marsh.

"I look at that harrier and feel sad that so many old-timers have no idea how priceless this place is," Bella said. "I guess having never lived anywhere else, they take for granted what the wide-open landscapes and wildlife do for their souls."

"I'm afraid that's human nature," Winkie said, "not appreciating what we have but wanting something else." She shook her head. "We reduce every decision to economics, not considering what truly makes us happy. People work their entire lives to get ahead financially. So they see change as progress. Laying down pavement and building houses seems the smart thing to do, the obvious path to a better life."

"Then I think when they're much older," Bella remarked, "a few find they're not really happy. They're surrounded by a world of fast food restaurants, tacky apartments, chain stores and trailer parks, and wonder if "that's all there is," as Peggy Lee used to sing. That's a pretty soulless world in which to raise children and grandchildren."

"Would it be any better if the Navy left?" Bill asked.

"Well that's the question that tears this island apart. The Navy is the financial engine that powers everything. I think with a change in the base's mission the growth would be more deliberate and the economy more diverse in many ways. We wouldn't have ear-splitting jet airplanes circling over the San Juan Islands, Olympic National Park and these last few places where we, and the wildlife, go for refuge."

Bill looked down at the ground and thought a moment. "I often reflect on what we've lost. It isn't real to most people because no one alive today was here then."

"What do you mean?" Bella asked.

"Well, we had a Gary Oak savannah with plant communities that don't exist anymore. One hundred fifty years ago the shoreline of Oak Harbor was a marsh that supported an entire food web of birds, fish and mammals. Of course the bay was full of salmon and shellfish. Native peoples lived around the shore for thousands of years. Now their bones lie bulldozed under asphalt streets, seedy taverns and second-hand shops. The Gary Oak savannah with its specialized wildflower community is now just a few tiny, broken remnants tucked into a small city park and behind a chain link fence in Navy housing."

"But," Bill added, "we can't go back. We can only go forward and try to save a little of what's left."

Bella's thoughts already had jumped ahead. Questions were forming in her mind about her friend, Father Benedict, and his ambitious building campaign for Our Lady of the Cove in Coupeville. Was Benedict's relationship with the Navy and the development interests closer than she realized?

In Bella's presence especially, Benedict made a show of loving nature. Some of that was a show for her, she sensed. Walking together he often pointed out common birds. But she'd seen this in others whose actual knowledge and interest were superficial. It was as if they were showing off their credentials, but in fact revealing how little they really knew by pointing out only the largest and most unmistakable birds on the planet, such as Bald Eagles.

He'd been a compassionate and attentive friend during the dark days of chemotherapy and uncertainty about her recovery. Bella would forever be grateful for that. But she had never heard him speak from the heart about the intrinsic value of all creatures, never heard him advocate simple humility and frugality, never heard him question material values.

This suddenly struck her as a curious omission in a Franciscan priest who answered to a Franciscan pope. The popular Father Benedict had breathed life into a failing Coupeville church – that was indisputable – and the community celebrated him for it. Now he was adding a new education wing that more than doubled the church's real estate. Capital improvements like that take money – a great deal of it – and it was coming from somewhere.

"Follow the money," she spoke out loud.

"What?" Bill asked.

"Oh . . . just thinking out loud. My mind's somewhere else."

"Well . . ." Bill said, "if you want to follow the money, here's a name for you – Dot DeGroot."

Chapter 10

Stu

Brad dialed his friend. "Bella is dead," he told Stu.

"Bella? I haven't heard that name in years. Whatever happened to her? Was she ill?"

"I'm trying to find out. Last I knew she was in Washington, D.C.," Brad said, choosing for now not to mention the mysterious email he'd received two weeks earlier. "Apparently she moved to Whidbey Island years ago for some reason, and semi-retired."

"What about that guy, her husband, the Syrian?"

"No idea. He doesn't seem to be in the picture."

Practically a hippie in Brad's estimation, Stu had been Brad's best friend since they roomed together at the university. Shorter and stockier than Brad, with a full beard, Stu wore his shoulder-length black hair in a ponytail. Brad knew they must seem an odd couple to those unaware of their long history. Their bond went back to the earliest confessions they'd shared as roommates. Those confessions led to a pact and, in a way, Bella was the inevitable product of it.

It started when Stu admitted he was miserable in high school.

"Growing up in Chelan, everyone knows your whole history, your family, and you have zero anonymity and freedom to become who you want to be," Stu said. "I didn't turn out for sports so I was always the outsider, never part of the circle of athletes and cheerleaders. You're not going to believe this but I've never even been on a real date."

"Me neither," Brad confessed.

Stu stared. "Seriously? This is the largest university in Washington, hotbed of liberalism and free love, and we're sitting here admitting neither one of us has ever been out with a girl?"

"I was a little sheltered in Coupeville. Mom was the church organist. Dad taught math in junior high and the kids mocked him behind his back."

"Oh man," Stu said. "That must have been hell."

"Yeah, and I was old man Haraldsen's nerdy kid. Our family were Baptist. I hated everything about it, all the hypocrisy, so I buried myself in books and just studied and kept to myself."

"Basically that was my life in Chelan, too. My parents ran a motel and I hung out as much as possible in the woods. I had some bad experiences I won't go into now. They were Catholic – full of guilt."

"Not much different than my people. But you know," Brad said, "that's all past. Now we're on this campus with 30,000 students who don't know us – half of them women – and there's nothing to stop us. We can be whomever we want to be."

"Well I'm serious," Stu said. "I'm tired of living on the outside. We've both got cars. That puts us way ahead. If you're up for this, let's start getting out around the city, maybe find girls who want to double date to some lectures, hockey games, pubs, go dancing."

"Double dating sounds good to me," Brad agreed. "I have zero social experience. There must be some girls in this building we could invite to our table at dinner. Everyone has a roommate, so if we get to know one, we'll get to know two. I don't see why we can't build a network and break out of this box we're in."

It worked. Step by step, Brad and Stu became insiders. People look back at their college years and say they were the best of their life,

Brad reflected. He wondered what they meant. Decades later they can tell you who was football coach and how the team did, as if it made any difference. But did those years really shape them as people?

For Brad what mattered was that he really liked the new person he became with Stu's help, and the close friendships they forged. Stu always maintained to Brad, "Being your roommate changed my life." It was the same for Brad also, and along the way it brought them to the attention of another journalism student, a shy Italian named Bella Morelli, who tested their bond but did not destroy it.

After graduation Brad and Stu both traveled by different roads to Idaho, where they continued to see each other. Stu became a reporter for the *Idaho Falls Journal,* where he met his laid-back wife, Amy, in the paper's newsroom shortly after breaking up with Bella. Brad spent four years in the Air Force in Idaho, then decided to stay and begin his newspaper career right there.

Stu was an avid hiker and angler, the quintessential outdoorsman and, improbably, a private pilot meticulous about the one thing that really matters to a pilot and his passengers – aircraft maintenance.

For Stu, Amy was the catch that didn't get way, the perfect match. She lived to camp and hike, and could sleep on rocks and clean fish with the best. It was obvious Stu wanted nothing to come between them. After his abrupt breakup with Bella and marriage to Amy, he had asked Brad less and less about Bella and soon stopped altogether. Brad assumed the dark and mysterious Italian really wasn't Amy's favorite subject, either.

Stu never told Brad why he ended the relationship with Bella so abruptly, but Brad knew. Bella told him in an intimate moment that Stu panicked and said she was uptight and the relationship just wouldn't work. They never had sex. Her college relationship with Stu, and the breakup, were high-profile news among their friends and humiliating for Bella. Her romance with Stu was perhaps the only public risk Bella ever took in her personal life, and it ended in rejection.

Brad never told Stu about his own relationship with Bella, what happened in the Gatlinburg motel, and that the three of them were joined in this other way, too. What good would it do? No one knew Bella had trusted and loved him, nor that Brad had never gotten over her.

To their friends, her name would forever be linked with Stu. They'd always remember her as Stu's ex-girlfriend from college, not Brad's.

Now none of it mattered. The three friends and rivals were suddenly just two. Years ago they had hurt one another in their clumsy fumbling to get something right. It had led nowhere, but the men's friendship survived. That bond mattered more than ever now since Brad's estrangement from Irene, and Stu's loss of Amy.

Amy had rolled her truck on a mountain road five years ago. Stu took it hard, gained weight and became a recluse. Brad, increasingly isolated within his own marriage, knew he wasn't far behind.

Despite the competition over Bella, Stu was the reason Brad settled in the potato state after completing military service – that and a job fell into in his off-duty hours. His personality profiles for the *Tumbleweed Times* brought him to the attention of *The Idaho Sentinel* in Boise, and Brad had spent the big years of his career there, before retiring with Irene to the ranch in Stanley. He had a way with people, a ready smile and a warm, human touch.

But sitting at that ranch would not tell Brad what happened to the woman he once loved, the one who might have changed his life, and why such a bright life ended 180 feet under a bridge.

"We should go to her memorial," he told Stu.

"Seriously? Bella is ancient history for both of us."

"Don't you think that's a little cold?" Brad challenged.

"Time moves on. Our lives went separate ways long ago. We can't change that she's gone and I'm not sure it'll do you and me any good to dredge up the past. I'm sorry about her death, but we're all holding a one-way ticket to the same place. I'm not feeling so invincible myself."

Brad let Stu's comment sit there a moment.

"By going we will honor her," he said, his voice breaking. "It's time to stand up and be counted." He was glad Stu couldn't see the tear roll down his face.

"This means a lot to you, doesn't it? I can hear it in your voice," Stu said.

"Yes," Brad said. "I feel some responsibility for letting her down. I think she was in trouble. Bella's death doesn't feel right. We need to ask some questions."

"What makes you say that?" Stu asked.

"She was not a quitter – we both know that. And the Bella I knew was fiercely Catholic. She believed suicide was a mortal sin."

Chapter 11

Father Benedict

Was the arc of Bella's life already set by the time she finished school in the late 1960s? Brad wondered. Looking back now with the perspective of time and geography, it seemed likely.

She did not show up anywhere on social media. If she had, Brad might have found clues to how the arc fell back to earth 50+ years later – what mattered in her later years, the friends, family, ideas, organizations and political views she held close.

Apparently she did not wish to be found by those from her past.

For a journalist she left a surprisingly thin trail online – a handful of major stories she had written for the *Washington Post,* ending in 2004 when she was still in her 50s, a decade ago. She apparently had few affiliations or activities that brought her into the public view or to the attention of search engines.

2004 must be when she left the East Coast for whatever reason and moved to Whidbey Island.

Brad found just one hit on Facebook, an event notice of a memorial to be held in two weeks, posted by Father William Benedict, a Catholic priest in Coupeville, Washington.

Brad clicked the icon for a private message and started to type.

"Father, did you know Bella? She was my J-school classmate in the 1960s. We

lost touch decades ago and I don't know anyone who kept in contact with her. I discovered her death by accident and did not expect it so young. Can you tell me what happened?"

Under his signature he added his phone number.

Less than an hour later, Brad's phone rang.

"Yes, Bella and I were close and yes, I was . . . stunned," Father Benedict began in an Hispanic accent. He seemed to choose his words with deliberation. His resonant baritone gave Brad the sense of a middle-aged man in vigorous health.

"She was a private person," the reverend explained. "Kept to herself. But I did not see this coming. She lived for that golden retriever of hers – Ida – short for Idaho, she said. Would you like a dog?"

Brad gulped. *Idaho?*

"So was it suicide?" Brad asked.

"So it seems. Deception Pass is the place of choice for that here. Every year we lose a few off the bridge. One of the tour boats found her on its first run of the morning."

"Did she leave a note?"

"No, just her purse and her Prius. That weekend she asked me to keep the dog for a couple of nights while she went away, but apparently she was planning this instead."

Father Benedict, it seemed, had known Bella since her move to Whidbey in 2004. Brad sensed Benedict was measuring his words, perhaps honoring confidences she had shared with her spiritual mentor. Brad pushed anyway.

"Was she troubled about something?"

Benedict hesitated. "She had her secrets and her troubles in the community – got embroiled in an ugly debate about the Navy's new Growler aircraft. That's a non-starter here. She'd be the first to admit she was an imperfect person. I think when she was young there were romantic involvements that did not end well. I don't know the details but often wondered if she ever got over those. More recently, yes, it's no secret that she battled breast cancer."

"Breast cancer? I had no idea," Brad said. "I wish I could have been there for her."

"I think cancer is the reason she left her job in the East. It appeared she won that battle or at least the first round, but all it takes to destroy hope is a bad follow-up with the doctor. We'll never know about that."

Benedict was the priest at Our Lady of the Cove. Brad learned Bella had sought his comfort during chemotherapy. Later, when she regained strength, they had often walked a popular bluff trail at Ebey's Landing and she had taken an interest in his work with the parish youth. He coached the church's Little League baseball team and drove the church bus to games in surrounding counties.

"Honestly," Benedict said, "I'm glad to hear from you because I just haven't found anyone from her past who knew her."

"What about family?" Brad asked.

"Her mother and father both died years ago. She was an only child and never mentioned any living relatives to me. Perhaps in the old country."

"And her husband?" Brad asked.

"What husband?"

Bella hadn't mentioned a husband, Benedict said, but it was surely her choice to leave that memory behind.

"Did she ever mention a child or a brother, a boy who would be 40 or 50 now?"

"No. Was there one?"

"I'm not sure."

"People move to islands for all kinds of reasons," Benedict said. "The psychology of island life makes this a good place to leave one's past behind, build a moat around oneself and start fresh in a sheltered community." He said Whidbey attracts loners and introverts because it's a small community where people can get to know one another slowly. The apparent isolation not only makes it easier to hide but, ironically, also easier to build new connections if one wants them.

He added that Bella's memorial would be an informal gathering of church friends at Admiralty Head Lighthouse, where he and Bella often walked. He expected a few members of the congregation would barbecue a salmon and some hamburgers and watch the sun set.

"It won't be an especially solemn or religious affair. You are welcome to join us if you can make it," he told Brad. "We'll toast her memory with a glass of wine. She'd like that."

Chapter 12

The Boy

Was there a darker side to Bella's friendship with the parish priest that he was not letting on? Where priests are involved, Brad thought, one wonders.

There had been a boy, Bella told Brad decades earlier. The boy's pain was never far from her heart and nearly broke her faith. She did not offer a name, but the long-ago story now was the first thought that came to Brad's mind. She had struggled with her faith, Brad knew. He wondered if that pain had come full circle somehow at the end.

In the story the boy, ten or so, was sensitive and quiet. His uncle, a priest, took a special interest, which led to a tortured secret the boy could never reveal. In a Catholic home a boy is no match for a priest's persuasion. "God loves you. God calls you to help ease my heavy burden as I deny my own physical and emotional needs for his glory and work."

The boy's sacred calling was to love and comfort his mentor, a special love the priest declared was the holiest and most godly there can be between a man and a boy. "You do not understand now," he said. "Someday you will, and you'll cherish what we shared. I would not ask if I did trust you as my own son."

And the uncle warned the boy that if he ever told the secret, he would shame himself, destroy his mother and father, and dishonor God, and burn in hell.

Chapter 13

Ault Meadows

In her red Prius, Bella cruised slowly up and down the residential streets of Ault Meadows, a new development of townhomes and duplexes just east of Naval Air Station Whidbey, also known as Ault Field. These were attractive homes for sale or rent, just off the approach pattern of the air station but within a 10-minute drive of the main gate.

The name was ironic. Meadows? Maybe there were meadows here before someone with a bulldozer improved the land. A meadow would be nice.

A young, crew-cut man in aviator glasses tossed a baseball to a boy in a blue-and-gold U.S. Navy T-shirt and matching ball cap. The ball landed with a smack in a mitt that seemed too large for the boy's tiny hand. The low sunlight of early evening glinted off the man's wire rims and gave everything a warm cast. The scene made Bella slightly sad about the family she never had. The aroma of burgers on the grill and the whack of croquet balls on manicured lawns completed the effect. This appeared to be slightly more upscale housing for officers and maybe some civilian employees of the base as well.

This neighborhood was much tidier than her own Admiral's Cove community, right under the approach of the Navy's outlying practice field. Yet in Ault Meadows, as at Admiral's Cove, many of the newer residences were listed for sale by Island Investors, Dot DeGroot's company. All of it was close to Wal-Mart, Home Depot and a who's who of fast-food restaurants. It was not hard to see how the economy worked in this place, nor what powered it.

From the newspaper, Bella knew the city was pushing hard to expand higher-density housing like this into county land currently classified as wetlands, farmland, forest production and light-density rural residential. In fact the county was doing all it could to water down wetland protections. Ault Meadows was perhaps a glimpse of what those outlying areas would become in a few years if the base continued to grow and the city continued to push outward.

And the Growler was the key to it all.

Islanders are of two minds about growth, Bella knew. The developers held that growth was necessary and beneficial – in fact inevitable – the engine that fueled higher property values, personal wealth, living-wage jobs and tax revenue to provide police and civic improvements. Drugs were a problem in the youth population and lay behind much of the property crime. More cops were the answer, many believed.

The other side held that nature was the defining difference in the island's quality of life, the essential attribute that made Whidbey Island unlike any other place and attracted people from all parts of the country to live and retire, including many Navy people. Salmon, whales, wildlife, hiking trails, forests and wide-open vistas made Whidbey Island a coveted place to live.

Clearly, Mrs. DeGroot and Island Investors had bet everything on growth and development.

The company's name had not meant anything to Bella until her priest, Father Benedict, mentioned Island Investors had made a huge contribution to the capital campaign for the church's new community building. She'd been curious who these investors were, and was dismayed when she found out.

What was it her California friend said? "Water flows uphill to money." On Whidbey Island, hearts and minds flow uphill to the Navy, which has the money. Noise was the price islanders paid for selling their souls, expressed in the signs one saw in front yards all over north Whidbey: *I (Heart) Jet Noise,* and *Our Aircrews Deserve the*

Best Training.

Everyone got their money from the Navy, and the Navy had enough to buy anything, especially the blind loyalty of those who wanted more.

Bella knew now what she was going to write.

Chapter 14

Kinship of Beings

"Right there – spyhop!" the naturalist shouted and pointed to a spot just off the port side of the boat.

Twenty people rushed across the deck to the other rail. A black-and-white orca was vertical in the water 60 yards away with its entire head above the surface, looking right at them. Bella felt its intelligence and curiosity, perhaps even an odd kinship among beings. Was she imagining this?

Camera shutters clicked up and down the line.

"Out-standing!" Billy Sizemore shouted. "Did you get that?" he asked Bella.

"I did," she said, "turning her camera so Billy could see the images in the LCD panel. I'll email them to you when we get home."

"Wow, wow, wow!" he declared as he scrolled through them.

Whale watching was Billy's idea and he was having the time of his life.

"It's his birthday Friday and he really wants to go whale watching," Fawn told Bella. Sarah's got something else and doesn't care. I told Billy we could take a guest and he chose you."

"So then I'm going," Bella said. "It's a date."

They'd been following the whales up the west side of San Juan Island, a favorite feeding ground of the local orca community, the Southern Residents. Here, off Lime Kiln State Park, the whales were lingering, breaching at times, seemingly playing to the cheers and gasps of their big audience on boats and many more watching from shore.

Bella had mixed feelings. A whole industry had grown up around whale watching, with dozens of tour boats from Washington and British Columbia converging whenever a few whales were sighted in the San Juan Islands or Georgia Strait. The whales could do almost nothing in daylight hours without an entourage of boats. The pressure on the marine mammals was intense, likely interfering with their ability to hear, hunt and feed. She knew the boat operators sometimes stretched the Marine Mammal Protection Act, positioning their boats ahead of the whales' direction of travel in tight passages so the whales would have to pass close.

"They came to us," the tour operators said. "We didn't chase them."

On the other hand, the tour boats gave many people their first and only real glimpse of these magnificent animals. Billy would remember this day for the rest of his life. If it opened the door to further learning about the marine environment, that was a good thing.

"We're going to move a few miles and it's going to get windy," the skipper announced over the intercom, so if you'd like to sit down and be comfortable, I'll put on some speed in a couple of minutes."

Bella, Billy and Fawn found seats on the upper stern deck, out of the wind and facing the warm sun. Bella took the break to tell Billy and Fawn a little of what she'd read about orcas. Many people know them as killer whales, she said, but they really aren't whales and aren't "killers" any more than humans.

In the past, some commercial fishermen viewed orcas as competitors for the dwindling runs of salmon. Giving these mammals an ugly name helped justify the practice of shooting them with guns. That all came to an end years ago when the public finally woke up to the truth and the federal government passed laws to protect them.

"Are they safe now?" Billy asked.

"Much safer than they were," Bella said. "At times in the past the Navy has used sonar in Puget Sound, which creates an ear-splitting noise under water, and this can hurt or even kill whales and other marine mammals. It seems to disorient them and sometimes drives them to beach themselves, trying to get away from the noise."

Fawn interjected, "That was a long time ago. Everyone loves the orcas now and wants to take care of them. We should talk about something more pleasant."

Bella sensed she had said too much. She wished it were true that the orcas were safe, but the recent buildup of Navy operations in the Northwest was very upsetting. The Navy proposed to carry out electronic warfare training over Olympic National Park and a large area of Puget Sound and the ocean extending off the coast, including the use of explosions and sonar.

Billy didn't need to hear that. Instead, Bella shifted to telling him more about the orcas themselves. They are more closely related to dolphins than to whales, Bella said, and the local resident orcas of Puget Sound eat only salmon. They seem curious about humans, certainly not hostile.

The naturalist on their boat today said the group they'd been watching were Southern Residents – locals – all members of the same extended orca family. There are other orca groups in other areas, such as the Transients and Offshores, and they sometimes pass through the Southern Residents' territory. The other groups eat a different diet, marine mammals such as seals and sea lions.

"Did you know orcas live about as long as we do?" Bella asked, "about 40 to 90 years. And orca families stay together for life. The Southern Residents speak a different dialect than other orcas and call to one another underwater. If there isn't too much noise from ships, they can hear these calls and locate each other from 10 miles away."

"So we live on the land our whole lives, and we have aunts, uncles, brothers and sisters, like my stupid sister," Billy said. "And the orcas do exactly the same right next to us in the water?"

"That's exactly right," Bella said, "except Sarah isn't stupid."

"Billy!" Fawn declared.

"I know. I just call her that. She calls me ignoramus."

When a single orca is born or dies, it's a very important change in the population, Bella said. There are only about 84 individuals in the entire Southern Resident community. There would probably be more if we had more salmon and our waters weren't so polluted with toxins and plastic garbage.

She wanted to tell Billy about the orca massacre that took place in Penn Cove, right near Billy's home, in 1970 and 1971, but decided against it. The story was too horrible to share with a youngster, especially on his birthday.

The entire Southern Resident Community was surrounded by boats and herded into the cove, where calves were separated from their mothers. Many were captured to put on display in marine parks. Many orcas died in the clumsy attempt to capture them. It was a devastating blow to the orca community. Most of the captured whales died soon after in captivity. The surviving Southern Residents and their descendants have never returned to Penn Cove since.

There is a lot to know about living in the Pacific Northwest, Bella thought. People are drawn to it every year, moving here in large numbers, never realizing how fragile it is. She wished more people were curious.

The world is full of givers and takers, she thought. The takers just want whatever they can get – clams, crabs, salmon, a performing whale, a treeless view . . .

The givers think about the tradeoffs, what it costs to enjoy such bounty, and what they can do to help preserve it for others.

Chapter 15

Dot DeGroot

"Ms. Morelli, a pleasure," Dorothy DeGroot declared, rising from her swivel chair behind the imposing cherry desk, bowing and smiling warmly. Tall and blonde, in an impeccable white pantsuit, she came around the corner to greet Bella, reached out and took Bella's hand with both of hers and looked right into Bella's brown eyes.

Wow, Bella thought. The rumors were true – she was polished. The commissioner seemed young and fit for her 60+ years, though her tired eyes belied some long nights and tough fights.

Stories swirled around Mrs. DeGroot and Bella had read many of them online before requesting this meeting. The commissioner's charm in public was legendary and a big reason why she was easily reelected term after term.

In private, she was known as the Iron Lady of Island County politics, a tenacious fighter and the only woman to sit at the Wednesday poker lunch of the Oak Harbor old boys' club, where the real government took place.

She was the female half of the island's foremost Republican couple with her husband Dutch DeGroot, mayor of Oak Harbor. Bella had heard she and Dutch even shared a celebratory cigar at times. She wondered if Dorothy didn't have aspirations to higher office, perhaps when the longtime GOP state senator in her district retired.

Bella looked around the room. A framed photograph on the wall showed a much younger Dot DeGroot shaking hands with a smiling Ronald Reagan, against a backdrop of US flags. Dot followed Bella's eye. "From my Young Republican days," she said.

Bella's gaze landed on a scale model of a Growler jet suspended in a 45-degree takeoff climb, on the corner of DeGroot's desk.

"Please be seated," DeGroot invited, stepping behind Bella and pulling out a chair for her, then tucking it in before returning to her own side of the desk.

Dot made small talk about the unseasonably warm spring weather and asked how long Bella had lived on the island, and where she was from. She seemed enchanted with Bella's whole life story and empathetic about her breast cancer. "That's always been my great fear," she confided. After a moment, Bella steered DeGroot back to the reason for her visit. "I don't want to take too much of your time so maybe we should dive in."

"Yes of course. What may I do for you?"

"I'm writing a feature story about the island's growth," Bella said, "and the controversy over the Growler aircraft. I'd like to get your perspective as a long-time county commissioner and investor in the community."

"May I ask for which newspaper?" DeGroot asked.

"*The Washington Post.*"

"Well my goodness, you do aim high. More power to you. This topic is a big one I wish more people understood, Ms. Morelli. May I call you Bella? This is a small community."

"Yes," Bella said, "and I'll call you Dot."

"By all means."

"What do you make of the divisions in the community over the jet aircraft noise?"

"Oh dear," she said, "that's really painful for me personally because I think the controversy is based on misunderstanding. All the bad press harms us as a community with the Navy. It pits people against each other and against their own self-interest in some cases," DeGroot said. "People move here knowing we are a Navy community, but a few of them begin to wish we weren't. That's not altogether playing fair in my opinion," he said.

"What about the argument that there are a lot more people than there were when the Navy came here, and the planes are a lot louder?"

"That's growth," DeGroot said, "and it's a positive thing. No one can stop it and that's as it should be."

"I live in the Growler flight path," Bella said. "Those low-flying jets at night are ear-splitting. They keep me up till 1 a.m. and cost me sleep and traumatize my dog."

"That's nighttime landing practice simulating the deck of an aircraft carrier," DeGroot said. "It's mission critical."

"Do they have to do it here, in such a populous area?"

"Well it does take a little getting used to," DeGroot replied with a compassionate smile. "But think about this. For 90 years until the 1940s Oak Harbor was a sleepy community of less than 1,000 people. Then the Navy arrived and in 10 years between 1950 and 1960, the population more than *tripled*. And then it *doubled* between 1960-1970, and *doubled again* from 1970-2000. Oak Harbor alone is a community of over 22,000 now and the Navy has brought prosperity and opportunities for all. That prosperity means more jobs, construction, houses, shopping and restaurants for the entire island."

"I understand the Navy promised the new jets, the Growlers, would not be any noisier than the Prowlers they replaced, and that there would be fewer of them. Many who live in the practice area say they are absolutely noisier, and the Navy keeps assigning more and more of them to the base."

DeGroot smiled. "I honestly see the Navy buildup as a good thing. The Navy is giving us a vote of confidence by investing in NAS Whidbey, and this is pumping more dollars into our community."

"Isn't it making the island economy unrealistically dependent on one employer? What happens if the Navy ever downsizes or leaves?"

"We had better hope that never happens."

"And what about your own interest in the Navy? You and your husband are real estate investors. Don't you have a personal stake?"

"Everyone does," DeGroot smiled. "Even you. If you own your home, or rent property, or shop at Big Box, or drive on our well-maintained roads, you can thank the Navy."

"Well, I've heard many in the community believe Big Box is actually a net negative for the local business community and taxpayer interests because it drives out competition and pushes down wages. Many of their employees are paid so poorly they require taxpayer assistance. But that's another story," Bella countered before shifting gears.

"What about the argument that the Growlers should do their touch-and-go practice somewhere else, in a less populous area of the state such as central Washington? As you yourself said, Whidbey Island is not the sleepy little place it was back in the 1940, before the Navy buildup. The community has changed, and so has the Navy and its mission, and its aircraft. Maybe the aircraft have outgrown the community."

"That thinking is not in anyone's interest – neither ours nor the Navy's. If the decision-makers in the Pentagon ever get the idea Whidbey Island doesn't want the Navy, the economic ruin here will be staggering."

"The concern about aircraft noise may reach further than Whidbey Island," Bella suggested. "Recently a report came out that the quietest place in the lower 48 states is the Hoh River Valley of the Olympic Peninsula, but the interval between episodes of man-made noise has shrunk since 2007 from an hour to about 20 minutes. What do you make of that in light of the Navy's plans to greatly increase electronic warfare training with the Growler jets over the Olympic Peninsula?"

"Times change," DeGroot replied. "It's as simple as that. Noise is the price of freedom. If we lose those jets, home values will plunge.

People will lose their mortgages. The banks will be left sitting on worthless real estate. There will be no jobs. Social services and county government will be bankrupted. If you think we have a drug problem now, wait and see what happens then! And there won't be any budget for police and sheriff's deputies to deal with them.

She kept going. "That's why it's so important people like you send the right message to the Navy brass in the Pentagon. I would go so far as to say I'm really asking for your help."

DeGroot rested her chin on her hand for a moment and stared at Bella, as if waiting for her to agree, then continued.

"Let me ask you something. Have you ever been hungry and dirt poor, Bella?"

"I'm not sure what that has to do with what we're talking about," Bella replied.

"Well, I know how it feels to be poor," Dot said, "and don't ever want to go there again. My parents were farmers back before the Navy, when there was nothing here."

"Ok."

"And the Depression came along and we wore rags to school and had just a few tough chickens to boil in a pot. Mom and Dad fought their way through those years and decided to roll the dice on the turkey boom. You've heard about that – the turkey era here on the island?" she asked.

"Yes," Bella said, "just a little."

"Poor Dad just couldn't get the timing right. He caught the end of the boom and then all of the bust. You know the turkey business on Whidbey just collapsed. And there we were again, on the bottom of the heap."

Bella waited while Dot fished a tissue from a box on her desk and dabbed her eyes.

Wow, she thought, this was quite a performance. "Do you need a moment?" she asked, playing along.

"No, I'm fine. Memories come back, you know," dabbing some more. "I'm just sharing, between us gals."

"So getting back to the Navy."

"When we got that darn bridge built and the Navy showed up at the beginning of World War II, things finally looked up. I swore I would never make the mistakes Mom and Dad did. I'd marry a man who used his brain, and by golly, that's Dutch. Lord knows he's not a perfect man by the farthest stretch, but he's a heckuva good partner. We've done well in real estate, but when you do well the risks just get bigger and bigger."

"I'm sure that's quite true," Bella agreed.

Dot continued: "Have you thought about what it costs to bring a real estate development to market? Millions of dollars. That's a frightening risk when you think about it."

"So," Bella replied, "we have two sides to this Navy noise controversy and emotions are high. I wonder if feelings are more heated than they need to be because each side feels the other isn't listening. Hearing your story helps me understand where you're coming from."

"Thank goodness for that," Dot said. Bella wasn't sure Dot would be so relieved if she had caught the irony.

"Does one side have to lose for the other to win?" Bella asked. "Isn't there a reasonable middle ground – a way to give the Navy what it needs while also being sensitive to those who desperately crave more peace and quiet?"

"You tell me if there is," DeGroot said.

"You don't have an opinion on that?"

DeGroot simply looked at Bella and smiled.

"Ok," Bella continued, "let's look at it philosophically. One could argue Whidbey Island's economy is way out of whack – almost entirely dependent on one employer. Is that a healthy condition for the county? There is also a health component to peace and tranquility. South and central Whidbey Island have an older population. As people age, more and more of them come under care for chronic, life-threatening illnesses. Have you ever been sick with a life-threatening illness, Dot?"

"No, the Good Lord has blessed me with very good health. But God, I hate the gym," she admitted, laughing.

"Well," Bella continued, "getting that close to death changes people. I nearly died a few years ago of cancer. I still don't know why I'm alive right now. That brush with death changed my thinking about what's really important. Sitting in the chemotherapy wing of the hospital I talked with a lot of other patients who experienced the same transformation."

She continued, "I talked with people who, as they grew older, became more reflective about the quality of their lives, the value of each day. The ones I've met walking trails, or watching birds, seem to immerse themselves in the wholesomeness and tranquility of nature. I know I'm not the only one who likes to listen to waves lap against the shore, and to the spring song of the Swainson's Thrush. I'm speaking from the heart here. My best times are when I'm out walking with Ida, my dog, watching her explore nature with sheer joy."

"We all love those things," Dot agreed. "I don't disagree in the least."

"To get to my question," Bella said, "do you ever wonder if we have been conditioned by our culture to measure prosperity and success falsely in terms of money and commerce and population? Are we making a mistake in thinking more of those things equals a better life? I wonder if there might be another way to look at it, a way that's more meaningful in the long run."

"Ms. Morelli, I honestly don't know what you are talking about now."

"Isn't there a huge value to nature, even a monetary value, that tends to get overlooked?"

DeGroot stared at her with a puzzled expression.

"I'll give you an example. I assume you've walked the shoreline trail around Oak Harbor Bay."

"Absolutely," DeGroot replied. "It's quite a jewel in the city's downtown revitalization and renewal."

"Well I'm sure you know the land on the city side of the bay once was a large wetland before homesteaders arrived and began diking and reclaiming the land for farming."

"Yes, those early farm families are a huge part of our city's legacy. Some of the land is still owned by the original families."

"And," Bella continued, "more than a century later, you probably know pieces of that land now are being transformed back to wetland and opened to the public as part of the city's trail system for walkers, bicyclists, joggers and birders."

"Yes."

Bella was getting a little wound up and knew it but couldn't stop herself.

"Because," Bella said, "it turns out, wetlands perform an environmental service as a filter for urban runoff, removing pollutants and toxins naturally before they can reach the bay. People crave places like that to get exercise and fresh air, relieve their stress, enjoy the birds and wildflowers, and renew their souls. It contributes hugely to the city's livability and economy. Boating and salmon fishing once were major recreational attractions in Oak Harbor, but there haven't been many salmon now for a long time."

"Well, there are many reasons for the decline of salmon," DeGroot remarked.

"Agreed. Lots of reasons, and they all add up," Bella said. "Restoring that wetland by Oak Harbor Bay is a piece of the solution. And at the same time it helps the city solve a terrible surface-water runoff problem that is costly and troublesome to manage any other way. You could pave that land and put a Costco or Wal-Mart on it, but in the long run doesn't it make more sense economically, and psychologically, to let nature make something beautiful there and do what it is so good at doing?"

"For the sake of argument," DeGroot interrupted, "let's say you're right about that particular piece of land. It doesn't change anything about the larger issue of development and prosperity for the rest of the island and its citizens."

"Well," Bella said, "I think there are some interesting aspects to this question. Every time a developer clears trees from a piece of land, levels it and builds houses, he creates a whole set of economic problems that weren't there before."

"Such as?"

"Development nearly always destroys a highly-functioning ecosystem. Trees and duff – the earth's groundcover – are magnificent filtration systems that help purify and regulate the release of water into the aquifer, on which we depend for our drinking water on the island. It takes centuries to develop that layer of organic material in the duff. Trees cool the atmosphere and restore oxygen. There's a real economic benefit to that. Trees are not a waste of land."

"You've read some books," DeGroot conceded.

"I talk to people."

Bella looked right into DeGroot's eyes. "Do you ever step back from all the development and commerce, and look at it that way?" she asked. "Are the fast food franchises and box stores and Growlers really enhancing your quality of life? Are they making our community a more wholesome place to live?"

DeGroot smiled. "Is that what you plan to write?"

Chapter 16

High Point

Looking out across Stanley Basin from his deck, Brad was thinking back fifty-two years to an evening in Bella's studio apartment in Washington, D.C. It was a night of wine and pillow talk that clinched the road trip that had changed Brad's life. Premarital sex was not on Bella's list of mortal sins – more of a gray area – though she did not embark on it lightly.

She was curious to see The Great Smokies. "I just have this romantic picture in my mind and want to go. My editor said he'd give me a few days if I came back with a story."

"About what?" Brad asked.

"I don't know. Gatlinburg is a pocket of privilege and fantasy for white newlyweds in a world that is burning with social injustice. I'll figure it out. All I want is a little piece of page 1 and a jump."

Brad laughed. "I wouldn't bet against you for that space. I've seen how persuasive you are with editors." The thought crossed Brad's mind that for Bella, sleeping with him would add realism to the piece she would write on the newlywed experience in Gatlinburg.

"Oh give me a break," she said. "Nothing is free, especially at the *Post*. If I write it well enough, I'll get the piece. I'll earn it."

"I know."

"And I won't neglect you while I do it."

Something had shifted between them. He could see it in her eyes, her smile, and the comfortable teasing.

It was in Gatlinburg that Bella trusted him enough to mention the boy – not who he was, nor where, nor when, but that the story filled her with rage, sadness, and a sense of betrayal. She could not go back and change that. But a journalist has tools, weapons if you will, to expose and stop the next betrayal. Brad sensed she was weighing whether to tell him more. Ever circumspect, she left it there.

They went on to happier things – the freedom of traveling together where no one knew them, what they'd seen, where they were going, and the euphoria of rehearsing a honeymoon they hadn't earned.

Just as Bella drifted off to sleep, Brad heard her mumble into the pillow, "You sure took your time."

During the night Brad awoke to soft sobbing.

"Are you ok?" he asked.

"This isn't research," she said. "I'm here because I want to be here with you."

It was the high point of their brief romance. He would leave the military in a year and go back to journalism. He wondered if their lives might yet converge.

To do that, one of them would have to give up something they loved.

But in the end geography did them in, as Brad feared it would. Neither of them gave up anything. After that idyllic week in Tennessee, he went back to the tumbleweeds of Idaho and the numbing emptiness of military life. Bella met a Syrian bureaucrat who worked in a federal agency in the nation's capitol. It happened fast.

"I'm seeing someone and I think it's serious," she wrote to Brad. "We're a lot alike."

Brad couldn't imagine what that would be other than olive skin, a brilliant mind and a sophisticated urban lifestyle and culture. He was probably not Catholic. To win Bella he must be brainy and handsome.

Within months Bella married the Syrian and they bought a condominium in Georgetown, where their life could not be more different from Brad's. Brad's world was mountains and meadows as far as the eye could see. Hers was museums and theatre and fine restaurants and taxicabs. They neither owned nor needed a car. The occasional, formal, handwritten note on fine stationery soon gave way to long silences.

Brad married a Boise woman who trained horses and embarked on the grand Western adventure that followed the lost years of the military.

Brad had barely paid attention to the Syrian's name. What was it, anyway, and where was he now?"

Maybe he'd find those answers on Whidbey Island.

Chapter 17

Dead Woman Walking

It was an unusually warm June evening. In the gathering twilight, Bella sat alone on a large drift log at North Beach on Whidbey Island, looking out at frothy white water churning through Deception Pass. As darkness deepened, the white rip current was the last detail she could see on the water's surface under the bridge.

The string of yellow headlights crossing the bridge seemed mesmerizing and reassuringly normal, she thought, people heading home at day's end to the comfort of families. She wondered how many of those people carried unbearable burdens as well.

Wood smoke from fire pits in the park's campground sweetened the atmosphere as she contemplated the next step. But one detail didn't fit – the revolting stench of a cigar somewhere close.

"Hello, Bella," came a woman's voice from behind.

"My god!" she jolted alert, rising from the drift log and turning toward the dark figure. "What are you doing here? You startled me."

"I'm sorry to intrude on your peaceful evening," DeGroot said, tamping her cigar against a log to extinguish it. A few red sparks jumped from it, and then it was gone. She put it back in her coat pocket. "For later," she said. "We need to talk."

"I don't think so."

"Walk with me," she insisted. "We have so much in common as two successful career women. I like you. Let's talk."

"No," she declared. "It's nighttime. I'm not going anywhere with you."

"Yes," she said, reaching into her other coat pocket. Bella's eye followed Dot's hand to the shape of a gun outlined by the fabric.

"Are you serious? You can't possibly think threatening me will solve anything at all. I'm not going."

"'Threaten' is a strong word. I really just want to talk, and it's important. This doesn't have to be unpleasant but we really must talk like two civilized people."

"How do you expect to walk anywhere in these woods in the dark anyway?" Bella asked.

"It's a good trail. I have a light. It's a nice evening and it's good to have some privacy. Dutch!" she called out. "Would you join us?"

Chapter 18

Bella's Island

"That's it. The gray one," Brad spoke into his headset, catching Stu's eye and pointing toward the aircraft's right side window. "You're almost over it now, on my side."

Stu dipped the wing for a closer look at an older bungalow with a weed-grown, fenced yard. The two-seat RV-14 was descending through Whidbey Naval Air Station's airspace right over Admiral's Cove, a shoreline enclave south of Coupeville on Whidbey Island. "That fence must be for the dog," Brad said. He had Googled Bella's address to see where she lived.

"Snap a few pictures," Stu suggested. "We are cleared with Whidbey Approach. Even though the Coupeville touch-and-go field isn't active today, we shouldn't linger. We'll swing out over Admiralty Inlet, west of the lighthouse, and let go of Whidbey Approach by getting under their airspace. Then we'll re-cross the island at Ebey's Landing to come in on the 45 for Eisenberg airfield by Penn Cove."

Brad noted the tall hedges of brush around Bella's house. "Guess I'm not surprised at the wild yard," he said. "She wasn't one to dig her hands into the dirt. Not that kind."

Stu laughed.

It had taken about four hours to fly some 600 air miles from Brad's pasture in Stanley, Idaho, but they'd stretched it into an all-day trip. Irene hadn't objected to Brad's announcement that he and Stu were going to Washington for a few days, to Bella's memorial. "Take as much time as you need," she said. "I'll be fine here."

Stu had flown the first leg alone, from Rigby to Stanley, where he picked up Brad. They had stopped in Lewiston for a long lunch and to top off the tanks before starting the dicey hop across the Cascades. In the mountains, clouds and fog can turn a short, straight hop into a long one.

Now the sun was low in the western sky, its golden tones flooding the marshes of Crockett Lake and the log-strewn beach at Keystone Spit. Brad noted a few people walking dogs on the brushy road that paralleled the backshore. In a few minutes they'd be on the ground just a few miles from where Bella had walked her last steps on Earth.

They'd catch a lift into Oak Harbor with some other pilot, rent a car, then double back to Coupeville. Since this was both a somber journey and a getaway, Brad had reserved rooms for them at The Captain Whidbey Inn. The century-old lodging would make a good, writerly headquarters for them with its creaky upstairs hall, rock fireplace and cozy bar. Brad had done his research. He knew the inn offered a soothing view of Penn Cove, where Master Joseph Whidbey of the Vancouver Expedition came ashore in 1792 to meet Salish villagers, whose longhouses rimmed the shoreline.

"Tell me again about tomorrow," Stu said.

"The memorial is tomorrow evening at the lighthouse," Brad said. "We should take a hard look at Father Benedict. I'd like to know more about him and his relationship with Bella, and retrace Bella's last steps. I'd just like to know how she came to this."

"What's your take on Benedict?"

"He appears to be Bella's only close friend. So far he's been forthcoming. I actually like him based on our exchanges by telephone and email."

"Never trust a man in a black hat," Stu said.

Chapter 19

Contradictions

Afternoon sun was just giving way to early evening as Brad and Stu parked by Admiralty Head Lighthouse, where a small group of adults and children clustered around three picnic tables.

Cheeseburgers sizzled on a Hibachi. Children squealed as they half-ran and half-fell sideways on the lush grass of the parade ground.

A tall figure in a black padre hat waited for Brad and Stu to reach the group at a gun emplacement marked Turman Battery. He nodded their way, then pulled a folded sheet of paper from his back pocket, studied it momentarily, and began:

Friends, we are gathered at sunset to honor our dear sister, Isabella Morelli. We remember her as a woman of great compassion, contrasts and contradictions," he began, his voice warbling. "*She was a gifted writer, generous in spirit, and a friend of our Catholic youth program and of men and women in uniform. She was also a private person we might say we never really knew.*

He launched into a summary of Bella's newspaper career and achievements, starting at the University of Washington and continuing through her many years at *The Washington Post*, where she reported on the national scene. Then he transitioned into her final few years on Whidbey Island and her prominent role with the youth of the church, with him as her mentor and spiritual guide.

"What a pompous windbag," Stu muttered. "I could do without this guy."

"You have a thing about priests," Brad remarked.

"Yeah I suppose I do," Stu replied. "Unfinished business."

Brad let it go. He was thinking about the hour and the waning light. As Benedict spoke, Brad tapped an inquiry into his smart phone.

"My god," Stu exclaimed, peeking over his shoulder. "You're checking tonight's sunset. Can't you ever just roll with it and be spontaneous?"

Brad wrinkled his forehead. "We have a couple of hours till we lose the light. Once that happens, these people will go home and we may never see them again. If Bella was murdered, there's a good chance the one who did it is in this group tonight. So whatever we can learn from these people, we have about that long to piece it together."

Bella loved men in uniform, Benedict continued, *so it's no surprise she specialized in telling their stories, and even as she battled cancer she continued to do so, writing about the sailors and airmen of Whidbey Island Naval Air Station.*

We all know now that Bella fought demons and private battles she didn't confide in us, Father Benedict continued. Brad leaned forward. *For some time she had struggled with depression. Whatever caused her to take her own life last month on Deception Pass Bridge, we know she felt it was her last, best hope to find peace and escape from pain in this life too heavy to bear.*

Stu wasn't paying attention. He was peeling back the foil from a jumbo-sized candy bar of milk chocolate and rice crispies.

"You're kidding," Brad said, nodding at the candy bar. "We've just arrived at a cookout."

"It won't spoil my dinner."

The view from this spot was the sprawling parade ground of Fort Casey and the backside of concrete bunkers, tunnels and cannon batteries dug into the earth, hidden from the shipping lanes on the water side. Half-a-dozen deer grazed obliviously, nearby. Two white-spotted fawns trailed close behind their mother.

Father Benedict concluded his remarks and walked over to introduce himself. "You must be Brad and Stu. Thank you for coming. Beautiful evening. This was the hour when Bella and I often walked on Sundays."

Brad nodded and reached out to shake hands. "She picked a peaceful place to spend her last years."

Stu kept his hand in his pocket and stared at something in the distance.

Benedict eyed Stu with a frown, paused, then picked up. "Indeed she did. We liked the fort for the views and the trail that runs down to the beach, as well as along the lip of the bluff to the north. Not too many people know about that bluff trail, but the twisted old trees are wonderful."

Fort Casey, he explained, was one of three WW-I Army posts on opposite shores of Admiralty Inlet that, in an earlier era, formed a triangle of fire. They were Puget Sound's first line of defense against foreign naval fleets that never came. Then at the outbreak of World War II, the U.S. Navy hastily built NAS Whidbey to defend Puget Sound against enemy submarines and its role has been expanding ever since.

The marine setting was so dramatic Brad momentarily forgot the real reason he and Stu were here. At the foot of this promontory, a white-and-green ferryboat accelerated away from tiny Keystone Harbor on a 30-minute run across Admiralty Inlet to the Victorian village of Port Townsend. Beyond the town lay the snowy peaks and sodden wilderness of Olympic National Park.

What a beautiful setting. Brad's eye was drawn just offshore, where the first of three cruise ships glided north in Admiralty Inlet toward the Strait of Juan de Fuca, just ahead.

"Alaska," Benedict said. "Several of them go past here in what's almost a convoy every Sunday evening in the summer."

Brad was daydreaming in the pleasant evening air, taking in the squeals of children toddling across the grass on rubbery legs. Kite-flyers walked backyards, raising their attack kites to catch the updrafts from the beach below.

"The only battles fought here any more are with kites and soccer balls," Benedict smiled, adding that little remains today of the mortars and canons that once filled the air with thunder. Out of sight within the bluff, machine guns waited to deal with any landing parties. The lighter guns were mounted aboard trolleys running out through steel doors to fire from the face of the bluff.

As they talked, a handsome young couple moved their way. Benedict introduced Brad and Stu to Navy Captain and Mrs. Steven Sizemore.

"Smokey," the captain corrected, reaching for Brad's hand and nearly crushing it as he pumped Brad's arm. Smokey's well-toned wife, Fawn, struck Brad as the Northwest outdoor type – tall, blonde, runner or hiker. Nearby were their two children, feeding pieces of hotdog to a golden retriever. Benedict identified the kids aloud as Billy and Sarah, ages 10 and 8.

"That's Bella's dog, Idaho," he explained.

"Can we take her for a walk, Father?" Sarah asked.

"Sure," Benedict allowed, giving the kids a knowing wink. Hang on tight to the leash and don't let her jump up on anyone."

Stu interjected. "I'll go with you if that's ok," he said to the kids. "Maybe you can show me the fort."

Brad watched his flakey co-investigator disappear into the distance with two kids and a dog. He would have to do all the work tonight without much help.

Several white-haired senior citizens talked at the adjoining table with a 40-ish brunette who laughed and smiled comfortably. Fawn explained the brunette was Jackie, one of Bella's oncology nurses at the island hospital. Given the older crowd and the conversation around Jackie, the occasion seemed a reunion of her patients.

"You're one of the classmates who flew in from Idaho," Jackie guessed as Brad approached her. "I heard you were coming. Maybe you can fill in some earlier parts of Bella's life we never knew. She was not only a patient to me but also a friend. But she didn't share much about the past."

"She could keep a secret," Brad laughed. "Well, she was two steps ahead of Stu and me as a journalist the whole time we were in school together. The Bella we knew was serious and private as a person, but a tiger with a story," he said. "She got all the choice interviews at the UW with national figures."

Then he added, "Could I have just a word with you alone?" They turned away from the picnic table and walked toward the bluff. Brad stared at the ground as he walked, forming what he was going to ask.

"There is some question in my mind about whether Bella took her own life or not," Brad said. "Did you sense she was depressed or upset?"

"Not at all. Normally I don't share patient information, but Bella is gone and that's just my opinion as a friend and member of her church. I'd like to know how she ended up under that bridge, too. Our conversations were quite casual and social while I administered the chemotherapy drugs and later drew blood for follow-up labs," Jackie said.

She continued, "Of course we don't always know what is going on in someone's life, but from a cancer standpoint it seemed her life was really turning around. She said her scans were clean. We were just doing the follow-up monitoring to be sure, making sure nothing came back."

"So you didn't sense she was depressed or had gotten some bad news recently?" Brad asked.

"If she had, I didn't see it. She seemed optimistic. She was writing and appeared pretty focused on something she was working on."

"Focused?"

"She looked tired the last couple of times I saw her. Said she had given up some sleep, putting hours into something. Didn't say what it was, just that she hoped she was wrong about a lead she was following, but she needed to know."

Over the months of Bella's outpatient treatment, she kept her spirits positive, Jackie said. Bella was never far from the Navy and was quite involved with the church youth playing softball and basketball, probably not only because they were kids but also because some were Navy kids.

"So her relationship with the Navy was close?"

"Yes if you mean on a personal level with the sailors and their families. Not so much on an official level with the military brass and Oak Harbor interests because she openly argued the Navy was covering up the true noise impact of its new FA-18 Growler aircraft. Ask Smokey Sizemore about that. She believed the planes were actually damaging to the human ear, especially the hearing of children, and devastating to the wildlife."

Jackie added, "Objecting to aircraft is not a popular stand on Whidbey because the Navy is so central to the economy. If you talk that way here you can end up hated and publicly condemned as unpatriotic. People don't want an honest discussion of some topics."

Brad noticed a middle-aged, shoulder-length brunette in faded blue jeans and a "Paws" T-shirt coming their way with plate of food, which she handed to Brad. "From the padre," she said. "And Amen to what Jackie just said. Imagine what those ear-splitting jet engines do to wildlife and pets. Animals can't escape it. I think the damage to animals is another issue Bella had with the Navy."

The Paws woman turned out to be Linda, a canine behaviorist who had helped coach Idaho through a rough period of reactivity and fears triggered by an abusive puppyhood. She said Bella had driven all the way to Moscow, Idaho, to rescue the dog from a shelter where many dogs were euthanized within days of arrival.

The Growler aircraft, Linda explained, practice touch-and-go landings at the Navy's outlying airfield south of Coupeville. Their flight pattern brings them low over the lighthouse and Keystone Spit, and Admiral's Cove, where Bella lived. The Navy assured the community that the new aircraft would be less noisy than the planes they replaced, but in fact they are clearly louder and there are far more planes and training flights. Many feel the noise, night and day, is intolerable and simply the worst it has ever been since the Navy built its Whidbey Island base during World War II, when planes were entirely different and quieter.

But it's even worse than that, Linda said. Now the Navy wants to use large portions of the Olympic Forest and Olympic National Park, and waters offshore, for electromagnetic warfare training. Areas will be closed to the public so military vehicles can transmit electronic signals and the Growlers can respond with simulated fire to take them out.

"Can you imagine what those jets will do to the peace and quiet of the pristine peninsula?" Linda asked.

The electronic signals are dangerous to humans and wildlife, so the Navy will attempt to exclude large mammals and people from its practice areas, but smaller wildlife and birds will be on their own.

"And if you say a disparaging word about the Growlers, you are mercilessly attacked as unpatriotic," Linda said. "You antagonize the big-money interests in Oak Harbor. The Navy is the goose that laid the golden egg for them in real estate holdings, and rich people give a lot of money to the church."

Father Benedict came in late on the discussion but agreed that Bella was troubled by the aircraft noise and the Navy's determination to push forward with the Growler. She'd written a couple of letters to the editor that generated sharp rebuttals from local reactionary types who lash back at everything. "Publicly, I stayed out of it," he said, "because it's my job to reach out to the whole community and keep politics separate from the church's life."

"What else?" Brad asked. "Was Bella troubled by health or other worries that might have driven her to take her own life?"

"I don't want to violate confidences," Benedict said. "Bella was a friend and I respected her privacy. I know there were things in her past, relationships and dreams that had ended in disappointment. I don't know the details. Deep down there was a sadness and secrecy about her I could never quite penetrate."

"What about family?"

"She had no living family I could find," Benedict said. "Her parents were deceased and she was an only child. I reached a complete dead end on that."

"What was her mood like in recent weeks?"

"Depressed about something, I would say. She stopped picking up the phone when I called, for one thing," Benedict said. "She seemed to isolate herself. She'd been quite involved in our youth athletic programs but pulled back. I knew something was wrong when she did that."

As Benedict spoke, Stu reappeared with Billy, Sarah and Idaho. Sarah handed the leash to Benedict and the kids headed back toward their parents.

"Thanks for the great tour," Stu called out to them. "That was fun."

"I'm glad you had fun," Brad said. "I've been learning a lot while you were playing."

"Me, too," Stu said.

Chapter 20

Captain Whidbey

Brad sat half-hypnotized under a patio umbrella at the rustic, log-style Captain Whidbey Inn. A warm onshore breeze rustled the Madrona leaves, lulling him and Stu as they shared their third round of Coronas and a heaping plate of cheese nachos and guacamole. Brad studied a bee as it crawled along the plate's rim.

They were waiting for a visitor who had agreed to meet them here. Neither felt the need to say very much, very fast. Brad was lost in thought anyway.

Perhaps if he had gone looking for Bella a few months earlier, things might have ended differently. It might be her sitting across from him on the deck today instead of Stu, talking about giving it another try. His mind wandered to that motel room in Gatlinburg, Tennessee – to the memory of her lying in his arms – and he smiled. Timing had always been their problem. In the last stage of one's life, after all the false roads of safe marriages and stable careers, what's to stop one from taking a risk?

Stu rested his elbow on the table and cradled his bearded chin in his hand. Brad had seen Stu's pensive pose before, when he was weighing what he was going to say.

"You were smiling," Stu remarked. "Nice to see."

"What? Oh. Daydreaming. I think it's an age thing."

"Did you love her?" Stu asked, staring down at his beer.

Brad hesitated, holding his glass with both hands and turning it slowly. "Yeah." Then, "Did you?"

"Yeah. But I knew the second we started dating that we would make each other miserable. I'm all over the road and an outdoor guy, and she was laser-focused, a neat freak and a city person, and a workaholic. She was an introvert and I needed an extrovert. I always knew deep down it was you she wanted in the first place."

"So when you made that move to go out with her, that was just to cut me off?"

"Probably. Wasn't it always competitive with the three of us?"

It pissed Brad to hear this, but why dwell on it now? That was 30 years ago and time had rewritten their lives. He and Stu had stood by each other through the decades. They'd shared pensive hours together around the campfire in the mountains. Friendship, like love, is complicated, and in older age friendship between men is fragile. Besides, time and selective memory dull the edges and blur the truth.

Stu looked directly at Brad's eyes. "We didn't do anything, if that's what you're wondering."

Brad said nothing.

Stu looked down at his beer. "You know I always envied you. I'm sure you had lots of girlfriends in all your years of dating before you met Irene. I don't know what happened between you and Bella, but I never slept with anyone till I met Amy and haven't slept with anyone else since, either."

"That astounds me," Brad admitted. "But it's funny that you envied me because I always envied you for Amy. You couldn't have found a more perfect partner in life."

Stu frowned, puzzling Brad. "It wasn't all smooth sailing. We had our problems, like everyone."

Stu said he thought Brad had won the lottery with his beautiful wife,

Irene, and her love of horses and dogs, and country life.

"Well it's pretty rocky," Brad said. "We have a partnership but it lacks a spark we just can't seem to find."

He could have told Stu about the week with Bella in the Great Smokies, but what was the point now? It would not bring them closer as friends, so he thought it should remain another of Bella's secrets, and his own, and maybe the better man knows when to keep his mouth shut anyway. Bella guarded her reputation. A friend honors that.

He couldn't escape the irony that Bella's love of urban places had discouraged them both from pursuing her romantically, and yet when she got down to the end of her life, she chose a small community on rural Whidbey Island as her home, and got a dog, and named her Ida for the state in which he and Stu both lived.

"Do you think she jumped?" Stu asked.

"I don't know. But I haven't seen anything to convince me she did, and I think if it was one of us under that bridge, Bella would want to know why, don't you?"

Stu nodded. "We owe her that and I owe you both something extra for the jerk I was."

Father Benedict had called Bella's death suicide. To Brad that was reasonable and plausible, given the long history of suicides at Deception Pass Bridge. But it struck Brad as a rush to conclusion, a curiously easy concession from a spiritual leader in a church that doesn't like to acknowledge suicide because it's a mortal sin. To commit suicide, Bella would have had to contradict her own Catholic faith.

"This mortal sin business you mentioned, is that a big deal in the Catholic Church?" Stu asked.

"Used to be, but I think they're easing on it, focusing more on understanding the pain that leads to such actions rather than condemning the individual."

"So it's not unthinkable that she jumped," Stu declared, "*if* she was in pain. And what I got from the Sizemore kids was that she might have been."

The kids, Stu said, were like Jekyll and Hyde. He found Sarah very social and easy to talk to, but Billy seemed fearful and sullen. "I don't think he trusted me enough to open up," Stu said. "Maybe the sullen thing is a phase boys go through if they have a macho, military father," he wondered aloud.

"The one thing I got out of Billy was an odd remark that he didn't want Bella to get hurt any more, and now she wouldn't. And what I got from Sarah is that Bella was seeing a policeman."

"A man in uniform," Brad mused. "Did you ask Billy what he meant about pain? Was the policeman hurting her?"

"He said Bella and Father Benedict yelled at each other."

It was clear both kids loved Bella, Stu said. They told him she was always checking on them and coming to their activities in the church's youth program. Sarah said sometimes the cop came with her. "I asked Sarah if she remembered his name but she didn't."

"And did you learn anything from the dog, since you're such a keen observer?" Brad asked.

"She loves those kids. But did you see when we brought her back to Father Benedict, she lowered her ears and tail?"

"Yeah, he's not much of a dog person and Ida knows it. But it was a nice touch for Benedict to bring her to the memorial," Brad allowed.

As they talked, Brad observed a trim, middle-aged man with a crew cut enter the patio from the bar and scan the crowd before heading directly toward their table. He seemed overdressed for the afternoon in khaki slacks, a blue shirt, red-and-blue striped tie and a navy blue blazer.

"Shane Lindstrom," he announced to Brad, extending a hand.

"How did you pick us out of the crowd?" Brad asked.

"The cowboy hats. You look like two guys from Idaho."

Brad winced.

Turning to the waitress who had followed him to the table, Shane said, "Just coffee please ma'am, black."

And he continued, "So you are reporters?"

"*Retired* reporters," Stu clarified.

"And you're writing a story about Ms. Morelli?"

"No, not at all," Brad assured. "We came for the memorial as two friends from long ago. I understand you're in charge of her file. We were Bella's classmates at the University of Washington in the 1960s. We're trying to understand how she ended up under Deception Pass Bridge."

"We see that a lot – several times a year," Shane said, grimacing.

"So it's officially suicide?" Brad asked.

The waitress returned and set down Shane's coffee, spilling a little in the saucer. He drained the spillage back into the cup, paused, and took a sip.

"Not just yet, but you know there are limits to what I can say, especially to persons outside immediate family. My interest in this is partly personal, not necessarily part of any official investigation. And I'm sure you know there's a lot I can't say."

"There's an investigation?" Brad asked.

"More of an open file. What I mean is that I have no reason to believe her death wasn't suicide, but neither have I closed the file. I'm still tying up a few loose ends. We don't spend a lot of time digging into people's personal lives unless there's a compelling question that points toward foul play."

"Isn't it unusual for the sheriff's department to assign a detective to a death like this?" Brad asked.

"It's a bit of due diligence. These bodies under the bridge are usually pretty straightforward," he said. "They don't take us away from other cases very long, and that's good because we don't have the resources anyway."

Shane explained that in Bella's case, he got a huge break, but one that actually makes closing the case more complicated. "The tide was apparently incoming when she hit the water because her body washed up on Strawberry Island, just inside the pass. So we have a body – a fresh one – and some questions. In most cases when the tide is outgoing we never see them again."

"Any chance she just slipped on a rock while walking and drowned by accident?" Brad asked

"Not with the internal injuries she had. Those came from hitting the water – hard."

Brad leaned forward. "I get the sense Bella touched off a firestorm with her opposition to the Growler aircraft."

"That's fair to say. I didn't agree with her myself."

"I saw a hateful letter in the newspaper a few weeks ago written by A.J. Ludke. Have you looked at him and others like him who were pretty worked up?"

"Ludke is a blowhard and a bully," Shane said. "He weighs in on everything, but I think it's all just hot air."

"Clearly Bella had enemies," Brad said.

"Yes she did," Shane agreed. "Our longtime county commissioner, Dorothy DeGroot, wasn't too fond of her because Dot and her husband own a lot of investment property. You've probably seen the signs for Island Investors. That's their company. As you can imagine, Bella's conflict with the Navy got under their skin. But I watch my step because Dot is my boss, since the commissioners control the budget for our department.

"She and the sheriff are pretty close," Shane said, "and I think it works to their mutual benefit."

"Close enough to . . .?"

"I've investigated enough murders to know the perpetrator isn't usually an enemy but a friend, a loved one. People say so-and-so is incapable of it. That's the one you have to watch. Put someone under enough stress and they can do anything."

Brad rubbed his forehead. "So it's safe to say Dorothy DeGroot wasn't one of those friends or loved ones you were referring to."

"Oh heavens no," Shane replied. "They were more like oil and water."

What in the world had Bella gotten into? Brad wondered. Shane slurped a sip of his coffee, then added, "The guy who can really tell you about Bella is the Catholic priest. He knew her pretty well."

Stu winced and rolled his eyes, but kept his mouth shut.

Brad explained they had met Benedict at the memorial gathering the previous evening. More people attended than they expected so it wasn't a good time to talk. They planned to sit down with him in a day or two, but wanted to hear the sheriff's perspective first.

"Do you think Benedict is on the level?" Brad asked.

"He's well respected. But yeah, when it comes to persons of interest, he was close to Bella and that makes him one of the people we have to look at."

"Did you turn up any indication of severe depression?" Stu asked. "Apparently Bella had quite a battle with cancer in the last 10 years and for all we know had gotten some bad news recently. What about Bella's doctor? Did you talk to her?"

"The oncologist. No, but certainly I know about the cancer and that would explain a lot," Lindstrom said. "When older people take their own lives it's often because of a bad prognosis. Bella herself was pretty open about her illness and the priest talked about it, too. Beyond that I can't say any more than to confirm what Bella herself told others."

Brad thanked Shane and asked him to keep them posted if he learned anything he could share. As Shane wove through the tables on the patio to leave, Stu turned to Brad and leaned his face close.

"Do you think that's Bella's cop?"

"Well if it is, the fact that we know is our secret for now."

Chapter 21

Explosion

The squeal of tires brought Bella running to her front window. A black truck was speeding away, leaving behind a cloud of rubber smoke.

Bella just caught the flash of yellow flame before a concussion slammed her house. Pieces of her mailbox rained down on the grass. She stood at the window, shaking, as her ears rang. Somewhere nearby, a car alarm whooped and warbled.

The monitor of her laptop glowed on the kitchen table with the beginning paragraphs of a story she was writing.

Special to *The Washington Post*

COUPEVILLE, Washington -- Dorothy DeGroot watches a Navy Growler scream low over the beach at Keystone Spit on Whidbey Island and sees jobs, growth and wealth.

Todd Carlson sees pain and terror. Carlson hugs his King Charles Spaniel tightly in his lap to protect its ears. He propels his wheelchair one-handed toward his parked car, several hundred feet away.

I was with Carlson one morning recently when two Growlers appeared.

"I come here often to escape all the weed eaters, pressure

washers and leaf blowers in my neighborhood. On Central Whidbey, I find wide-open spaces to enjoy the quiet and listen to birdsong, and recharge my mind. It's psychological therapy for my war injuries."

Carlson, a decorated combat veteran of Operation Iraqi Freedom, suffered permanent spinal cord and nerve injuries on his tour of duty. And mental health effects.

"I came home broken," he said, "both physically and psychologically. I couldn't admit the invisible injuries at first, but found I always felt calmer after a few hours in a place like this. The wholesomeness of nature, watching the animals go about their lives, helps me heal.

"So a place like this is a refuge for you?" I asked.

"Yes, when it's quiet. I rest and reconnect here," he said. "It's the one thing that brings me peace and relief from the pain and bad memories for a little while.

"Can you imagine what this ear-splitting assault does to the birds and wildlife? They have nowhere to hide, no way to protect their hearing. Many birds hunt with their hearing as well as their eyesight."

Champions of the Growler and its noise sometimes label opponents unpatriotic, even soft on terrorism. Carlson argues the issues aren't that simple.

"This airplane is wrong for this setting," he said. "It's not a question of loving your country or not loving it. People feel embattled by an intolerable noise assault."

Noise here from the Growlers has been measured at 134 decibels. Anything over 85 can cause hearing damage with repeated exposure. At nearby Rhododendron Park, children play where measurements of 115 have been recorded.

County Commissioner DeGroot brushed that aside when I met her at the Navy's outlying landing field near Coupeville on another recent morning. "These are our American flyboys," she shouted over the shriek of jet engines straining against full flaps as the planes touched down, then jumped into the air again. "Doesn't that make your heart pound? Best in the world. They're the reason this island is great, and doing great."

NAS Whidbey's new Growler electronic warfare jet is arguably the noisiest aircraft ever based on Whidbey Island. And since the base was built in World War II, the numbers and loudness of its aircraft have steadily increased.

When the Navy announced it was deploying the Growler to Whidbey, it promised the jets would be no noisier than the ones they replaced. Instead, they turned out to be noisier, and there were more of them.

Now the Navy wants permission to conduct low-level training flights with the Whidbey-based aircraft over pristine reaches of Olympic National Park.

For DeGroot, now serving her seventh term as county commissioner, the Growler is the reason she and her husband are multi-millionaires. They are the aircraft's foremost cheerleaders and defenders on Whidbey Island. That's the part of the story everyone sees.

But there's another part, a darker side, DeGroot and the Navy don't want you to know. It's about sex, money and pow . . .

Chapter 22

Benedict's View

If anyone could shed light on the last decade of Bella's life, Brad was pretty sure it would be Father Benedict, who described himself as Bella's closest confidant during the years of cancer, chemotherapy and self-imposed exile.

When Brad had approached Benedict at the memorial about a sit-down talk, the priest suggested instead they do it this evening on a three-mile hike of Ebey's Landing and Perego's Lagoon. The trail is a favorite of the local community and of Bella, he said. It follows the rim of a high bluff with expansive views of the ocean on one side and acres of black, cultivated prairie on the other. At the halfway point, the trail descends to the beach and many hikers make the return trek at sea level, along the shoreline of a brackish lagoon.

"I do my best thinking while walking," Benedict said. "And you should see Ebey's Landing anyway before you go back to Idaho."

But neither Brad nor Stu was thinking about returning home before they'd put together a clearer picture of the circumstances surrounding Bella's death.

Ebey's Landing sounded like the perfect place to get some fresh air and exercise while also learning what Benedict could tell them.

Brad and Stu arrived early at the trailhead for the six o'clock hike and used the extra few minutes to sit on a large drift log and watch the surf crash ashore. The beach here faced west toward the Strait of

Juan de Fuca and the open ocean. While Brad stared at the horizon, Stu ran his hand through the polished stones within arm's reach. By the time Benedict drove up in a black Toyota Corolla, Stu already had found several agates and slipped them into his pocket.

The priest unfolded his tall, angular body from the car and reached back to the passenger seat for an old-style padre hat with a razor brim. The hat looked sharp, Brad thought, on a lean, silver-haired man obviously fit from lots of hiking. Together with Benedict's neatly pressed black shirt, the hat made a pretty clear statement that he was clergy. The effect struck Brad as slightly intimidating, though he was relieved the priest was wearing jeans and comfortable walking shoes.

Stu walked over and peeked into the car. "No dog today? I'll bet Ida would love this," he said, waving his arm toward the trail.

"What?" Benedict remarked. "Oh . . . no, not today. I thought it would be easier to talk without her."

After one final check for water bottles, the three headed up a steep trail toward the rim of the bluff above. Minutes later they emerged, winded, on a plateau of farm fields. Brad drew alongside Benedict and asked how he met Bella.

She showed up at the Coupeville church about 10 years ago, Benedict said, when the prognosis for her cancer looked pretty tough. The oncologist had given her long odds of beating it but kept her hopes alive, and Bella was reviewing her life and questioning what was important to her. Surgery and chemotherapy were exhausting and she often felt weak, taking naps at all hours. She had to avoid public places at busy times to minimize exposure to people and their germs, especially children. She complained of chemo brain, simply not being able to think or make even the smallest decision.

"Do you see that hawk?" Benedict asked, jolting the conversation back to the moment. "Red-tail. We get them all the time here. Bella and I did a lot of bird watching. She knew more about them than I did."

Resuming his story, Benedict said he soon realized Bella had no deep ties in the community, no family or close friends. "She was hiding out," he said. Even her home was somewhat isolated and overgrown with hedges of Nootka Rose, and no immediate neighbors, so the church was her lifeline to the community and her source of comfort.

He started visiting her at home and taking her on short walks on Keystone Spit just to boost her spirits. "She developed quite a love of wildlife and nature," Benedict said. "I think it was calming and soothing to her when all those poisonous chemicals were circulating through her bloodstream. She loved the early mornings – before sunrise – when the world is just waking up."

Brad couldn't help reflecting how much alike he and Bella had grown, unbeknownst to each other.

Benedict added that as time passed and Bella completed chemotherapy, her energy improved and the walks became longer. She decided she wanted to become involved with kids and that's how she started helping out with the church's youth athletic programs.

"Did you sense any particular sadness in her, Father?" Brad asked.

"Well to be honest, yes," Benedict said. "Like all of us, she was getting older and feeling the challenges of age more and more. She'd never found the contentment of a lasting relationship. Her career had peaked and essentially ended. She'd fought a tough battle with cancer and was holding it at bay, but can you ever drop your guard? Then she waded into the controversy over the Navy's practice field and incurred the vitriol of many in this community."

"Hey speaking of that," Brad began, "did she ever mention Dot DeGroot, the county commissioner?"

"Everyone knows Dot," Father Benedict replied. "She and her husband, Dutch, are a long-time members of our parish, well liked in the congregation and in their elected positions in the community. They're the first to help whenever we need anything."

"But they and Bella . . . ?"

"Not close friends, I don't think," Benedict said.

Brad said Bella's conflict with the Navy was no surprise. When he knew her in the 1960s she was quite anti-war. Maybe the Growler fight suited her in a way – to oppose the plane while standing up for the airmen and their families.

"She was a person of contradictions, yes," Benedict said, with a smile. "Apparently she did a 180 from her anti-war days at some point because the Bella I knew was infatuated with uniforms."

"Speaking of uniforms, did she mention she was seeing a policeman?" Brad asked.

Brad noticed Benedict stiffen and purse his lips. "Nope. That's news to me."

"Yes, that's what we hear," Brad said.

"I guess it wouldn't surprise me. Exactly what did you hear about it?" Benedict asked.

"Not much – just an offhand remark someone made," Brad replied, keeping it vague. "Do you think it might have been more than a friendship? Could she have been despondent about a relationship that wasn't going well?"

"Maybe, but she was such a private person, it's hard to know. I would call sometimes, knowing perfectly well she was home, but she wouldn't pick up the phone. I felt her sadness was more about the accumulated disappointments of a lifetime – early love interests that didn't work out, the end of a career that had provided her only sense of purpose, and then aging and cancer, and conflict with the community."

Brad nodded. He wondered how much Benedict knew of Bella's history with him and Stu. Was there more to Bella's feelings about that than she'd ever shared with him? Had she told Benedict some key piece that would explain a suicide?

Stu jumped in. "Father, you said Bella was involved in the church youth program. What was the story on that?"

"Oh just the usual volunteer support," Benedict said. "Maybe a bit of the surrogate mother thing. She drove the church van to some of our events. She encouraged the kids, took an interest in their schoolwork and such. Modeled the Christian life. The kids liked her.

Chapter 23

Goose Rock

Only one other car was parked in the North Beach lot when Benedict arrived in late afternoon. He got out of his Corolla and inhaled the invigorating forest air, stretched his calf muscles on a log rail nearby, then put on a down vest and a Mariners baseball cap and started his hike, which took him under the bridge to the rocky headlands on the other side of the highway.

The walk to the summit of Goose Rock was an easy half-hour trek from this parking lot, which was usually deserted at this hour of day. He and the person he was meeting had chosen this place and time so there would be as few others as possible who might recognize them. He passed no one on the trail, and when he finally emerged atop the rocky bald, only one other person was there, a pudgy man in dark glasses and a visor, in hiking shorts, sitting on the granite outcropping with his back to the trail, watching Growlers fly their patterns in the evening haze at the Naval Air Station.

"Dutch, I barely recognized you in that alpine get-up," Benedict declared.

"Well that's the idea, Padre," Dutch replied with a chuckle. "In – cog – neet – o."

Benedict held out an arm and leveraged Dutch to his feet. "Where'd you park?" Benedict asked. "I didn't see your car."

"Over on Cornet Bay Road. I came up the back way, but I swear that's the last time. Those switchbacks nearly killed me."

Benedict gave him a friendly squeeze in the crotch but Dutch backed away. "Goose Rock," Benedict pointed out with a smile.

"Jesus, Padre! We've got to talk some business," Dutch said. "What's going on with these two farmers from Idaho?"

"Nor farmers – reporters."

"Whatever. Are you making sure they keep their noses out of places they don't belong? The Growler is one thing but if this other . . ."

"They're harmless," Benedict said. "I'm guiding their inquiries. Nothing for you and your wife to worry about."

"Well, worrying is what gets us reelected. Jeeesus, we're under pressure."

"What do you mean?"

"The governor is all over us to tamp down this Growler business. So is the base commander. And our friends in Congress aren't too happy about the letters in the paper. I just got off the phone with Senator Blanchett, who reminded me this is a sensitive time for the base and our state. He called the publisher, too. If those country boys stir this up any worse, life will get complicated for us all. Dot and I are not letting that happen and I don't think you are, either."

"By the way," Dutch added, "I'm sorry about your friend, Bella. Sorry you had to do that."

"Do what?" Benedict asked, staring at the ground. "I think you know a lot more about it than I do."

"Aren't you the sly one?" DeGroot shot back. "Let's just leave that where it lies."

"Something else," Benedict said. "I can't keep meeting you like this. The risks are too great, so this is the last time."

"Don't be so sure about that," DeGroot said. "If you think the risks are great for you, imagine how great they are for me. I encourage you to think a little more about who your friends are. Keep them on your friendly side. Now about those potato people, how much longer are they going to hang around here?"

"Another day or two I'd guess," Benedict said. "They just need a little more reassurance that Bella took her own life. I'm making sure they get that without being obvious about it."

"Well, if you can get them out of here soon, perhaps I could slip a little more into the collection plate and something on the side to your own retirement fund, as well."

"Much appreciated," Benedict said, taking Dutch's hand. The two walked arm in arm toward the bushes.

"Now, dammit, I've had a hard day and am full of stress. So appreciate this," Dutch said, loosening his belt and dropping his pants.

"No way!" came a young voice somewhere in the brush.

Chapter 24

Break In

That evening over beers in the Captain Whidbey pub, Brad raised the uncomfortable question that had been on his mind ever since their talk with Shane Lindstrom. If Bella's digging and poking had threatened a county commissioner's major real estate holdings, and if she had close ties to both the Navy and the sheriff, was the truth about Bella's death buried under pretty tight wraps?

Brad banged the table with his fist, a little harder than he intended. "Damn it anyway," he said, his head buzzing from one too many beers. "Either there's nothing to find – just a straightforward suicide – or we're looking in the wrong places."

"Then I think we're going to have to get inside Bella's cottage," Stu declared. "If she was in trouble or digging into the wrong things, the answers probably are in her computer."

"That means breaking and entering," Brad said. "Are you comfortable with that? 'Cause it's crossing a line."

"No, I am not," Stu replied. "It's not what I do. We may be interfering with a sheriff's investigation or implicating ourselves in foul play, but that's where we'll find answers."

"Providing the computer isn't missing or wiped clean," Brad countered. "If Shane suspects something, he's probably seized it by now. And if he hasn't, someone else may already have covered their tracks. But if we find signs of a cover-up, we'll know for sure someone needed to cover something."

Since Bella's death had been high profile in the news, Brad said neighbors probably would be more alert than usual to any activity around her home. He didn't think they should risk driving up to the house and parking, for example, and they absolutely shouldn't go there at night, turning on lights. Instead, he suggested they approach the cabin on foot in the early morning, dressed in sweats as two older men out jogging.

They knew from their earlier fly-by that the cottage was somewhat screened from view by neglected landscaping and hedges of wild Nootka rose, but entering someone's house without permission was well out of their comfort zone.

"The part that worries me is whether we can get in without breaking something and making it obvious someone was there," Brad said.

"Let me handle that," Stu replied. "Amy was always screwing up and locking us out of the house and car, and leaving the keys inside. I have some modest experience in this area."

*

By 6:00 the next morning they had left their car a quarter mile away at Driftwood Beach and started their jog up Keystone Avenue to Bella's shoreline community.

Two doors from Bella's cabin they passed a dark brown vehicle parked nose-out in a driveway. "Oh Christ, that's a sheriff's car," Stu remarked. The vehicle had condensation in the windows, indicating it had sat overnight. "A deputy must live there."

It crossed Brad's mind that Island County Sheriff's vehicles were the most aggressive looking police cars he had ever seen, as if built to impress a teenage boy. It was something about the color of mud, blackwall tires and open grille.

"Just be cool," Brad urged. "Deputies have to live somewhere."

At Bella's driveway, they ducked behind a dense hedge and went around back of the house where they would not be visible to cars and passers-by. Stu pulled a set of thin, plastic gloves from his pocket, plus an extra pair for Brad. "Just a precaution," he said. "I saw this in a movie. We'll try some windows first in case any are unlocked, but we'll probably have to go in through the back door. Looks like an easy lock anyway," he said, nodding toward it.

Bella must not have been too worried, Brad thought, because the lock was just a simple, twist-style, doorknob. After Stu confirmed the casement windows were all locked, he pulled a putty knife from his pocket and inserted it between the doorframe and the knob to push back the beveled latch. Then he pulled on the knob and the door opened neatly, revealing a cheerful porch and sunroom. Even in the predawn, the room had an uplifting feel.

In a corner sat several ceramic bowls arranged neatly on a placemat.

"Ida's dishes," Brad said.

Ferns in large pots and hanging baskets drooped from neglect. "I'd water those plants," Stu said, "but we aren't really here."

On the oak kitchen table, Brad noted a half-empty cup of tea next to a basket of mail and a small calculator. He idly sifted a few letters – medical insurance summaries, lab reports and aging bills for long-finished radiation services – before continuing deeper into the house and finding Bella's office in the den.

"It's here," he announced to Stu in the other room. "Her laptop. I want to see who she was emailing and also look at her files and search history."

While the computer booted up slowly, Brad suggested, "Why don't you check messages on the answering machine?"

Stu found the machine and hit *play all*. It beeped and a disembodied voice declared. *"No messages."*

"Nothing," he said. "Everything's erased."

Meanwhile, Bella's computer had awakened to a black screen with a box in the center and a blinking cursor: "Password."

"Damn," Brad said. "It's password-protected. That's all we need – to sit here and guess at it."

"We're screwed," Stu said over Brad's shoulder.

"Not necessarily," Brad replied. He typed a few keystrokes and hit "enter." Nothing happened.

He typed a few more. Still nothing. And a few more . . . and the whole desktop lit up with icons.

"How did you do that?"

"It's almost always the dog or cat's name. People often add a number to it to make it harder, so I added a 1," Brad said as he opened Bella's email.

"Now this is interesting. Her inbox is totally empty. Someone deleted everything – either Bella or someone else." He clicked some more. "So is her email." Next he clicked on trash.

"Ahhhhhhh," he declared. "They just moved everything to trash but didn't empty it. Whoever deleted all those emails didn't know much about computers." Brad clicked down the list for a moment. "I see several here from Father Benedict that she didn't answer," Brad said. "The latest is, 'We need to talk. Give me a chance to explain.' And look at this, several from our detective friend, Shane Lindstrom."

"'I'll be over tonight,' he wrote. 'Marie is attending a workshop in Seattle.'"

"So she was in touch with Shane?" Stu asked. "He sure didn't mention that."

Brad quickly scanned Shane's last several emails. "He seems to be a neighbor. That must be his car in the driveway two doors down. He says here that he'll keep an eye on the house and park his car more visibly. Apparently she'd been the target of some mailbox vandalism, spray paint and drive-bys over her position on the jet noise. Shane says the vandalism is probably the work of some lowlife inspired by a high-profile right-winger in Oak Harbor, our friend Ludke, but he'll need to catch the perpetrator in the act."

Brad opened Bella's Firefox browser and clicked on the "History" tab, then "Show All History."

"Well," he said, "whoever got into Bella's computer didn't know how to delete the search history, either, because it's all here. Lots of searches on the Navy's EA-18 Growler, as you'd expect. She was also reading about cancer and nutrition, Catholic doctrine and the assignment of priests to various parishes in New England. And lots of news articles online – New York Times and Washington Post, especially."

"What are the articles?"

"Little of everything. War in Iraq and Afghanistan, Pentagon cost overruns, county government, canine reactivity, pedophilia in the Catholic church, military spending, Congress, the Stanley Basin . . ."

The last one caught Brad short. Whether from idle curiosity or something more, she had clicked on an article about Stanley, Idaho, where he lived. They'd had no contact for decades, but in the last days of her life she was apparently thinking about him.

"Keep an eye out the curtain," Brad said. "I have just a little more to do here and then we should get out."

He slipped a 20 megabyte jump drive into one of the USB ports, found Bella's document files and copied them all to the memory stick, turned off the computer and watched it power down.

"Ok, we're out of here."

As they pulled the porch door shut behind them and stripped off the plastic gloves, Brad felt relieved they had left no traces. But as they started back to where they'd parked at Driftwood Beach, he noticed the sheriff's car next door was missing.

Chapter 25

An Unexpected Knock

Three hours later, Brad and Stu were hunched over Brad's laptop in an upstairs room at the Captain Whidbey when a knock on the door startled them.

Brad got up and answered. "Detective Lindstrom," he declared. "This is a surprise."

"Yes, I expect it is."

Brad's heart was in his throat. Did Shane suspect something? Brad invited the detective to sit in a wing-backed guest chair as Stu angled the laptop away from his view.

"You were up early this morning," Shane observed. "Think I drove past your rental car at Driftwood Beach."

"Yes, trying to get back to some exercise again," Brad laughed, patting his abdomen. "I'm surprised you recognized the car."

"Oh, it's my job. I ran the plate and the rental office gave me your names. Most of the early birds out at the beach are regulars, so I was curious. But the reason I'm here is to ask if you've satisfied yourselves about Ms. Morelli's death."

This was bizarre, Brad thought. Shane clearly knew more than he was sharing, and was fishing to see what they knew. Was he looking for the truth or trying to cover it up?

Brad stared at his hands. "We've got nothing, detective. Had a long talk last night with Father Benedict and he described Bella as isolated and melancholy, but to me it doesn't add up to suicide. It may be exactly that and nothing more, but that isn't how it feels."

Shane stared straight into Brad's eyes. "Then maybe we should both lay our cards on the table. What did you find in her cabin?"

Brad reeled but met Shane's stare and came back with a question: "Why didn't you tell us you knew Bella pretty well before her death?"

"Fair enough."

Shane explained he met Bella a few months ago, after she called the Coupeville office with concerns about vandalism and her safety. Since he and his wife lived so nearby, he talked with Bella and promised to stay in close touch and keep an eye on her home. Even with their 15-year age difference, her breathy voice and mysterious quality were seductive to him, and he felt flattered that she seemed to like him, too. She made him feel young and attractive to women again, and it was not a burden to look out for her, he confessed with a nervous laugh. "I looked forward to her calls and emails, maybe a little more than I should have."

He said his proximity seemed an immense relief to Bella and they grew to appreciate each other beyond a strictly professional basis, more as friends and confidants. "We did not sleep together, if that's what you're wondering," he said.

The room went quiet and Shane looked down at his lap. "But God, I loved her. And miss her."

"So as her friend and confidante," Brad began, "what was really weighing on her mind?"

"She wouldn't say!" Shane exclaimed. "Obviously she was embroiled in the jet noise controversy over the Growler. It brought her plenty of grief, but just about everyone on Whidbey Island is involved in that controversy on one side or the other."

"Was her cancer back?"

"I don't think so. No. She had grown philosophical about death anyway – really didn't seem to fear it. She would have told me, I'm pretty sure. But you haven't answered my question, 'What did you find in her cabin?'"

"Probably what you already found, too," Brad said. Her answering machine was clean. Email and browsing history were deleted, but not very successfully, because whoever did it only moved them to trash. I'm surprised you didn't seize her computer."

"I downloaded everything," Shane said. "Left the computer as bait in case someone came back. I've been watching the house pretty closely and put a webcam on the sunroom."

"Holy crap," Stu said, throwing his arms in the air.

Chapter 26

The Bridge

Standing on the narrow sidewalk 100 feet from the south end of the bridge, Brad shouted to Shane over a stream of oncoming cars and trucks. The bridge shook especially with each gravel truck, and Brad was surprised how many there were. The windblast of the trucks and whine of their tires just three feet away unnerved him.

He wondered how much flexing an old structure like this could take, decade after decade.

"Twenty thousand a day," Shane shouted over his shoulder, nodding toward the oncoming traffic as he led Brad single-file toward center span.

"Sorry, what?"

"Twenty thousand vehicles a day cross this bridge. Imagine how different it was in 1935 when this bridge was built for the traffic of the Great Depression. Whidbey Island was the boondocks then."

"By the way, that's the boat that found her body?"

Brad watched a high-speed tour boat emerge from under the bridge, trailing a white wake, on its way out.

"It runs on the hour," Shane said.

Logging trucks, motor homes and tractor-trailers streamed across the bridge while tourists ventured timidly on the narrow sidewalks with cameras and iPhones, unable to take their eyes off the scene below. The whole situation made Brad uneasy. He didn't care for heights, and the beauty below was both mesmerizing and terrifying.

Green water swirled in eddies and whirlpools as it rushed under the bridge. The outgoing tide was running fast. The scent of fir and hemlock trees, mixed with gasoline and diesel, wafted in the spring breeze.

"So your partner is chasing down another interview today?" Shane asked.

"Yes, the Sizemores. Saturday is a good day for that because the Sizemore kids are home from school."

Brad explained that ever since meeting the Navy family at Bella's memorial, Stu had wanted to talk some more with them. The kids' mother, Fawn, had said it would be fine for Stu to stop by today.

"Any idea where Bella might have stood before she went over the rail?" Brad asked Shane.

"Not really. Probably on this main span rather than the shorter Canoe Pass. And at least this far out to miss the rocks, so she'd land in the water."

"No one saw anything, I take it," Brad said.

"No, and you can see how busy this bridge is. To go over the rail with no one noticing, you'd pretty much have to do it at night when things are quieter."

"How did she get here? Where was her car?"

"That's interesting," Shane said. "The park ranger found the car at North Beach, a short hike away. There's a trail from North Beach to the bridge, so it's quite doable, but jumpers don't usually take such an indirect route like that. They park at either end of the span, or just stop in traffic at mid-span and run over to the rail. Maybe she was out hiking and didn't necessarily plan to jump till she got here."

"But you don't believe that," Brad stated.

"In my heart, no," Shane said.

An answer from the heart is not what Brad would expect from a cop, but he kept in mind that Shane lived on her street and had said earlier that he loved her, whatever he meant by that. She had a certain mysterious quality men liked. It wasn't a burden to look out for her, Shane had said. Though Shane was married, he admitted he looked forward to Bella's calls and emails perhaps a little more than he should have. Was there more to Shane's interest than he was sharing?

"That railing is awfully low," Brad pointed out. "It makes me nervous just standing here."

"Honestly," Shane said, "you could grab someone's legs from behind and give them a little lift and off they'd go. It would be that easy."

The tide apparently had been incoming because Bella's body had washed up on the rocky shore of Strawberry Island, a obstruction in the channel just east of the bridge. Shane said wind and rain had prevented the local tour boat from operating for several days. When tours resumed, someone spotted the body on the first run of the morning while scanning the shore through binoculars for Harbor Seals.

"Could you tell how long she had been there?" Brad asked.

"Several days, according to the coroner."

"And her injuries?"

"Lots of broken bones," Shane said. "We think she hit the water chest first because nearly all her ribs were broken and internal organs punctured. If she was conscious at all after hitting the water, it wasn't for long."

"Could she have been dead before she went over the railing?"

"Possibly," Shane said, "but there were no suspicious wounds. No head injuries except what you'd expect in a fall like that. She had a little water in her lungs maybe from a reflexive breath, but they were also punctured by ribs, so that's inconclusive."

He continued, "Hey since I've got you alone today, there's something I've been wanting to ask you."

Brad nodded his ok.

"Any idea why Stu flew a round trip from Rigby to Snohomish the weekend of Bella's death?"

Brad recoiled. "He was here in Washington?"

Shane nodded. "For a couple of days."

"He didn't say a word to me."

"Those two airports are both un-towered so there wasn't much of a paper trail except that he flew on instruments and the whole trip was mapped on flight-tracking software.

"And you checked this?"

"All I needed was the tail number. I'm just curious about the whereabouts of everyone who was part of Bella's life. If someone helped her over the railing of this bridge, it was probably someone she knew."

"So you've looked at me, too?"

"Yeah, I made a couple of calls. You were all over the Stanley Basin that weekend, attending community meetings and a workshop for dogs with fear and reactivity issues. You left a pretty wide trail."

But Brad wasn't listening. He was racing through the reasons why Stu might have flown almost this identical route from Idaho to Seattle the weekend Bella died and not said a word about it.

Brad had seen nothing in Bella's email to indicate she'd been in touch with Stu, but that wasn't surprising because Stu rarely used email anyway. He was a pick-up-the-phone guy. Neither Bella nor Stu used social media, so there would be no trail there.

Shane broke the silence.

"Could there have been any unfinished business between Stu and Bella going back to when they dated after graduation?"

Chapter 27

The Gatlinburg File

Brad was stunned. Stu had flown here the weekend of Bella's death. Brad would need to confront Stu, but would choose the moment. Something else was on his mind, as well – something he had not yet discussed with either Shane or Stu.

Poring over the files from Bella's computer the previous evening, he'd found something that jolted him like an electric shock. It was an unassuming sub-folder buried inside another folder misleadingly titled "Household misc." His eye went right to it because of the folder's name: "Gatlinburg memories."

Had she left this for him, if he ever got this far?

Gatlinburg would mean nothing to Stu but it screamed at Brad. If Stu questioned the name, he'd say Bella must have picked the most irrelevant name she could dream up for the folder.

But the significance tormented Brad. Had Bella titled it as a red flag if something happened to her? She could not possibly have foreseen he'd ever be in a position to find it. More likely she did it simply to conceal what she was working on in case the wrong person came snooping.

Brad saw immediately it had nothing to do with Gatlinburg but was largely about Argentina. The files included links to dozens of articles and websites:

- Argentine church allegations of sexual abuse, 1994, against 47 seminarians
- Seminarian Raphael Benedicto testifies against Argentine priest
- Pope Francis defrocks Argentine priest
- Pope's action hailed, but was it enough?
- Jpeg. 47 seminarians
- Jpeg. Seminarian in padre hat
- Predator priests shuffled around globe
- Cycles of abuse repeat from generation to generation
- International priests and the charter for protection of children and infants
- Foreign priests help in US shortage
- U.S. Catholic Church relies on foreign-born seminarians
- Coupeville parish welcomes new priest from New York City

Brad clicked on the second jpeg. The handsome young Argentine seminarian bore a striking resemblance to Father Benedict. The padre hat was a dead ringer.

Chapter 28

Fawn

It was Stu's idea to split up and pursue two tracks in the investigation of Bella's death. Ever since meeting the Sizemores at Bella's memorial he felt there was more to learn from the Navy family.

"Whatever was going on with Bella, the Navy was a piece of it," he told Brad. "The Sizemores no doubt saw her through entirely different eyes than Benedict did."

When he called the Sizemore home and reached Fawn, he found her surprisingly warm. "Oh absolutely, hon', I'd love to visit some more," laying on some Southern charm. "You doll. I think you passed Billy's test," she told him over the phone. "You seem to have the same gentle, nonthreatening energy as Bella."

"Well, I see a lot of myself in your son, Billy," Stu said, certain that Fawn had no idea what he really meant by the remark.

The Sizemores lived just a few miles from The Captain Whidbey in the Sierra community. All the houses were view homes with attractive, suburban yards facing the Strait of Juan de Fuca and Victoria, British Columbia, on Vancouver Island.

Fawn answered the door in color-coordinated pink yoga pants and sweatshirt, her blonde hair tied up in a ponytail.

"Ta-da!" she declared, arms outstretched as if making a grand entrance. "Sorry about the get-up. I'm multi-tasking with the vacuum cleaner today."

While the kids played in the back yard, she invited Stu to sit and talk over a cup of fresh coffee in the sunlit dinette. The aroma of those beans, plus a cloud of cinnamon wafting from the oven, was irresistible.

"Could I interest you in a cinnamon roll?" Fawn asked. "I think I remember from the memorial that you have a sweet tooth."

"Was it that obvious?" Stu asked. "For crying out loud, yes. Is this what it's like to be Steve, waking up to fresh cinnamon rolls each day?"

"Yeah, I'm a goddess," Fawn laughed. "You have to be, to stay married to a Navy pilot."

This flirty woman seemed oddly out of step with the humorless Virgin Mary watching over them from the wall as they drank their coffee in the breakfast nook.

"Steve is flying touch-and-go's today, and then going to the rifle range with his friend A.J. So he said to give you his regrets, and his best. It's my gain. I have a distinguished gentleman caller all to myself."

"Touch-and-gos?" Stu asked. "So that would be . . ."

"Field carrier landing practice. He's an instructor pilot in the Growler."

"Holy crap!" Stu exclaimed. "What a thrill! Must be like riding a rocket. I fly a smaller plane, which is how Brad and I got here from Idaho. But cripes, Bella's opposition to the Coupeville training flights must really have rubbed Steve the wrong way."

"Well of course," Fawn agreed, nodding decisively. "And A.J. is like a dog with a bone. He's always gnawing on something or someone. I don't think he was such a good influence. The Growler controversy was a sore point between Bella and Steve."

"A.J. sounds familiar for some reason."

"He writes letters to the newspaper."

"So he and Steve are buddies?"

"They're both really into guns," Fawn said. "Makes me uncomfortable. Frankly, I wish Steve would find a friend who golfed or built model airplanes. I guess it's all part of the macho thing about noise and explosions."

"Would you say Steve was pretty upset with Bella about her Growler position."

"Yes and no," she said. "Steve and Bella argued but it wasn't exactly personal. He liked her as a person but not her politics. That's the great thing about Steve. He can compartmentalize and disagree and then move on. Bella liked our kids and for that reason Steve liked Bella – we all did. Billy invited her whale watching with us and it was the best day of his life."

With Bella out of the picture, Stu wondered if Fawn was giving him a revised and sanitized version of the relationship, so he pushed a bit more.

"Do you think she was trying to drive the Navy out of Whidbey?"

"Omigod no, I never thought so at all," Fawn said. "But she was pushing the Navy to change the base's mission. If she had closed down that Coupeville touch-and-go strip, it would have cost my husband his job and probably forced us to move. We weren't happy about that."

"But you know," she continued, leaving the sentence unfinished.

"What?"

"Well, Bella had a point about the Growler noise. It's worse than any plane Steve has ever flown."

"Was that Steve's opinion, too?"

"It would be a career-ender for any Naval officer to admit it, so don't ask him and don't ever quote me. Steve knew Bella had a valid point. He just didn't want her, or anyone else, talking about it."

Honesty was always Bella's strength as far back as Stu could remember, he said. It seemed like Fawn had a touch of the same quality.

"So what was Bella saying?" he asked. "That the Navy shouldn't train its pilots?"

"Well that's how A.J. frames it. But I think Bella was saying they should move that carrier practice to a less-populated area, such as Central Washington. The whole economy of Whidbey and the neighboring counties is built on the Navy, so obviously the town and the Navy brass don't want to hear anything that jeopardizes that."

Fawn shifted the conversation over to Stu, saying she was curious how Stu and Brad had ended up here at Bella's memorial. So Stu filled in the story of the three friends and their tangled love lives.

"And you all lost touch with one another for the last four decades?" she asked.

"Somewhat," Stu said. "It was Bella's choice. Brad and I ended up settling in the wild west of Idaho and marrying rural women. My wife died in a car accident and Brad is having some challenges in his marriage. I don't think Brad ever stopped being in love with Bella. He was in the process of looking her up when he discovered her death."

"Oh no, what a mess. That's not good. What about you?" Fawn asked. "Had you gotten over her?"

"Oh yes, I think so," Stu said. "But not over the guilt of what I did to Brad and her. If I hadn't stepped between them when I did, they might have ended up together."

"You can always second guess yourself," Fawn said. "It's all hypothetical and leads nowhere."

"I feel an obligation as a friend to stand up for Bella now that she can no longer represent herself. That's why I'm here, really," Stu said.

"And what else am I going to do now that I'm retired? I just hunt and fish."

Stu said he noticed on his walk with the kids that Billy seemed pretty sullen, guarded and quiet. It surprised him. Sarah was much more outgoing. He wondered if Fawn and Steve had noticed that, and when it had started.

"Billy's been withdrawn for some time – a year or so," she said. "He's taking Bella's death hard. I've wondered if it was a reaction to Steve's gung-ho, military cockiness," she laughed. "You know how these hotshot pilots are!"

"Oh yeah, like me," Stu laughed.

"Exactly," she laughed.

"And we have our fights," she added. "Billy is pretty sensitive and I know it upsets him, but when stress breaks out between two adults, you can't always shield a child from it."

This was pretty forthright talk. Stu was thinking it was just as well Steve wasn't home today, sitting across from an old hippie in a frayed sweatshirt, with a backwoods beard and disheveled hair. Brad and Steve would have a lot more in common than Stu did with Steve, in light of Brad's military training and discipline. So maybe it was just as well Stu had timed this visit when Steve was away.

But he thought Fawn seemed quite comfortable with him, and he was enjoying a pretty woman's attention.

"Bella was very nurturing and I think Billy felt safe with her when the church teams played sports. "

Stu was agonizing whether to take this comfortable conversation to an uncomfortable place.

"Well since you brought it up, I have to ask about your take on Father Benedict."

"Brilliant man. He's a leader in the community and sits on the board of every charity and civic group. He is devoted to the church and his work as priest," Fawn said. "He's done a lot to build up the church's role in the community here. We joined because the Coupeville church is so engaged, with strong youth programs," she said.

"No," Stu said, "I mean what do you think of him personally?"

"Makes quite an impression," she said. "Tall and fit, and very bright. He may not be as warm and fuzzy as some. He's more of a theologian than a hold-your-hand shepherd of the flock, if you want to put it that way," Fawn said. "Some call him a bit remote or formal. He loves the rituals of the church."

Stu's thoughts were drifting to another revered cleric, a powerful man who wrapped himself in a holy cloak of respectability. He had invoked God as his leverage over a young boy a lifetime ago, and not till decades later did the boy understand the pattern plays out generation-after-generation.

He could still hear the twisted words. "As our Holy Father's representative on Earth," Stu's uncle said, "I took a vow that even your own father did not." The speech was beautiful and finely crafted. "I have denied certain physical needs to serve God. You are too young to understand, but you will one day. God has brought you into my life and into his service to comfort me as I do His work. This is the most sacred and loving gift you can give our Lord. I would not ask it unless I loved and trusted you as completely as my own tender son."

Yet their secret seemed shameful and dirty. Stu's uncle insisted such matters are the most personal, beautiful and private moments that ever pass between two people in the world – the highest and purest, most godly love there can be. The family would never understand, and Stu must never mention it. No one would believe him if he did, and he would only spite God, betray the church's holy representative on Earth, shame himself as a liar, devastate his parents and destroy his uncle's entire lifetime of good work.

So Stu had withdrawn into himself, confused and afraid. He only regained a measure of confidence after he entered college and broke free of religious guilt, partly from hours of examining religion with his atheist roommate. Like Brad and Bella, Stu chose the introvert's profession of journalism, but for entirely different reasons. He never told his private secret to even his long-time friend, Brad.

But in an unguarded moment, he did tell one person, Bella.

The secret of his life was one of the reasons he'd sat out the sexual revolution of the 60s. He also thought it was probably the reason he never had sex with Bella.

Stu's consciousness returned to Fawn's kitchen. He didn't know how long he'd been away.

"I don't know how to ask this delicately . . ." Stu began.

"You think Father Benedict's a pedophile?" Fawn blurted. "Absolutely not."

"You're quite sure."

"He's a friend of our whole family. Absolutely a stand-up guy. If you saw how compassionately he cared for Bella when she had cancer, you could never suggest such a thing."

"Those are two different things," Stu pointed out. "People sometimes show different sides in different circumstances."

"Well that's a side that doesn't exist. If you're looking for someone who might have meant harm to Bella, it's not Benedict but these right-wing gun nuts."

"Fair enough," Stu said, feeling it was time to lay this topic to rest with Fawn, though he was far from done with it personally. He couldn't believe he hadn't even had to say the word; it was Fawn who brought it up.

Chapter 29

Majed Sulieman

Penn Cove shimmered in the soft light of late afternoon as Brad relaxed on the Captain Whidbey's patio and angled his laptop to shade the screen. His stomach growled for dinner but a cold beer mellowed the day's edges nicely. The waitress had disappeared and he didn't have the energy to get up and find a menu. Then again he didn't need one. He wanted the burger, not the creepy shellfish that made this place famous.

He struggled to focus as he opened folder-after-folder of mundane files he had downloaded from Bella's hard drive.

Then in a folder titled Grocery List he got lucky – the details of Bella's marriage, plus photographs and divorce decree, emails and personal letters she had scanned. This was so like Bella to hide things, Brad thought, recalling when he visited her apartment in Washington, DC, and she retrieved a $20 bill from the pages of a thick book on her shelf.

She had married Majed Sulieman in 1985 and divorced him in 1995. It appeared a colossal failure – the mistake of a lifetime. He had emigrated to the US from Raqqa, Syria, and qualified for his green card by marrying Bella. The green card jump-started his fast track to citizenship, and soon he had landed a comfortable US government job with the Office of Fair Housing and Equal Opportunity. Brad opened a subfolder of correspondence between them and started to read.

"You do not understand Islam and never will," Sulieman wrote. "I had high hopes for you as a woman of faith. You of all people should understand. Instead you disappoint me. When we married I felt sure you had an open mind. As the head of our household it is my decision where we will live, and after all the pleasant talk between us, it is a wife's duty to obey."

Sulieman, it seemed, had briefly flirted with American secular ways when he first moved to this country, then been drawn back to his Islamic roots. He came under the influence of fundamentalists at a mosque in Washington, D.C. By the mid-1990s he had reached a decision to return to Syria, and expected Bella to go with him. She would not.

"I have been patient. You have returned my patience with insolence. What happens now is the will of Allah the Merciful. I wash my hands of you and your slutty, infidel, American ways."

Brad wondered what that meant. He cradled his head in both hands, rubbed his temples and stared at the words.

*

"You look like you're deep into something," came Stu's voice as Brad's friend pulled back a chair and joined Brad at the table.

Brad grimaced. "Getting the story of Bella's husband."

"Seriously?"

"It's all here in Bella's files. They divorced in 1995 after he went back to Islam and apparently returned to Syria."

"Amicably?" Stu asked.

"Not so much. His tone in these letters is pretty bitter."

"There was so much about her we never knew," Stu said. "Why was she always so damn secretive?"

"She was always concerned about appearances," Brad said. "It's how she was raised – never to gossip, never to say an unkind word. I never knew her to discuss what she considered private matters with anyone, not even friends. I'm sure her failed marriage was a source of much pain and profound embarrassment."

"So we still don't know if Bella committed suicide or not. But assuming she did not," Stu said, "our list of suspects has now grown by one more. My own list includes Father Benedict, Detective Lindstrom, Smokey Sizemore, some nut in Oak Harbor named A.J. Ludke, the whole U.S. Navy, and now an Islamic fundamentalist ex-husband who may, or may not, have gone back to Syria."

"And there are some other loose ends," Brad said.

"Such as?"

"You for one. I have to ask, why did you fly to Snohomish the weekend Bella died?"

Stu's face turned ashen.

"Who says I did?"

"Shane Lindstrom. He checked your tail number on a flight-tracking website."

"Holy crap," Stu said, throwing up his arms. "Shane! It was a personal matter," he added softly, avoiding eye contact. "It's nothing that concerns Bella or what we're doing here."

"I think I need to know," Brad insisted, looking Stu straight in the eye.

They sat in silence for half-a-minute. Stu looked up, looked down, cleared his throat.

"I'm having some medical issues," he said at last. "A doctor in Idaho Falls referred me to a colleague at the Seattle Cancer Care Alliance – the big alpha doc. It's outside my health plan but Mr. Big owed my Idaho doctor a favor and agreed to talk with me on the weekend. He's the top guy in leukemia. So I came here to get another opinion on what I should do."

Brad reached across the table and touched Stu's hand. "How bad is it? What's the prognosis?"

"Depends on luck and which treatment I choose," Stu said. "The chemotherapy is harsh and probably won't work. There is a gentler approach that skips the poison and builds up your system, and every so often it works and adds years of quality time. But it's complicated. There are pros and cons. I haven't decided which way I'll go yet but at least now I understand the choices."

"I wish you'd told me earlier," Brad said. "I'll help you any way I can. You're not alone on this."

"I appreciate that. I didn't know what to say, or exactly when. I'm pretty spooked. When you called me about Bella, she went to the top of the agenda. I didn't want my problems to get in the way of your search. We can come back to it after we finish with Bella."

"Let's not push it aside," Brad said. "Neither of us can do anything to bring Bella back, but you're here in front of me right now, and my best friend in the world, and I will stand with you no matter what."

A deep rumble in the distance grew louder. Brad and Stu paused to watch two dots come toward them low over the water.

"Growlers," Brad declared.

The jets shrieked past the inn at eye level as diners covered their ears with their hands and some ran for the inside. The sound was ear splitting.

"Is that normal?" Brad asked.

"I don't think so," Stu said. "Somebody's hot-dogging on the way to the Coupeville practice field."

"Yeah," Brad said with a smirk. "It's the sound of freedom."

"Funny you should bring it up," Stu said. "What I got from Fawn is that her husband had some pretty big differences about this with Bella. Fawn claims he kept them in check and liked her. They are a Catholic family and Fawn lets on that she really loves her husband. But she was also awfully flirty. There may be some cracks in the marriage not easily visible on the surface."

"So how do we break this thing open?" Brad asked.

Stu leaned back, raised his beer glass and studied the amber color. "Put pressure on Benedict."

Chapter 30

Pressure

"Where's your friend today?" Father Benedict asked when Stu showed up unexpected at his office at the church.

"We split up sometimes to cover more ground. It's getting harder to make sense of Bella's death, so we decided we need to move a little faster." What he could have added, but didn't, was that they were trying the good-cop, bad-cop routine, and Stu was the bad cop.

Benedict smiled. "I'm surprised you're so troubled by that. What happened seems clear, but if there's anything I can do to ease your worries I'll be only too happy."

Stu cut in, "You can. I'm curious about how you came to Coupeville."

"I'm not sure how this concerns Bella, but like many of my brothers in the priesthood I studied in Latin America. Priests move around, and with the shortage in the United States the church transferred me to New York City, and from there to Coupeville."

"By Latin America," Stu interjected, "you mean Argentina."

Benedict stiffened. "Yes, if it matters."

"Did you know that in 1994, an Argentine priest was defrocked in a sexual abuse scandal involving 47 seminarians?"

Benedict's face reddened and a large vein in his neck stood out and pulsed. He pulled a hankie from his pocket and dabbed it at his forehead, all the while glaring at Stu's eyes.

"I've heard about it," he said tight-lipped.

"And that you appear in a group photo of the 47 victims?"

"That was a painful time, but why bring it up now? It's ancient history." Benedict scowled. "I could not let that stop me from the work of the church, and I haven't."

"Psychologists say there is a pattern in abuse cases – that the victims sometimes go on to become perpetrators themselves."

"I think you have crossed way over the line of ordinary decency."

"And I wonder if Bella brought up this question with you, herself?"

"I have no further comment," Benedict said. "This is outrageous."

Chapter 31

Pushback

Brad loved early mornings. They were his favorite time for photography and he remembered Bella liked the early hours, too.

In mid-May, the sun rises over Penn Cove about 5:30 a.m., starting with a single spear of intense orange bursting around some peak in the Cascade Range. Long before this the sky passes through three successively brighter shades of twilight. Each has a name – astronomical, nautical and civil twilight.

Two hours before the burning orb rises into view, while the sun is still far below the horizon, its first rays begin to insinuate their way dimly into the landscape. Reflected off the atmosphere, they alter the darkness ever so subtly with the first vague hints of shape. This is astronomical twilight.

Brad had been up since 4:00, sitting by an open, second-story window that faced out toward the glassy cove, just barely visible on this moonless night. He was scrolling through documents on his laptop. Something had awoken him from a light sleep, some movement next door, maybe Stu getting up to use the bathroom. Once Brad's brain started working he couldn't shut it off, so he was spending these quiet hours looking deeper into Bella's diabolical system of mislabeling files. The soft glow of a desk lamp was all the light he needed or wanted.

A loud *craaack* startled him, just as the mirror behind him exploded.

Glass showered down in a heap on the dresser and grit sprayed out across the room, pelting the back of Brad's head.

He dove for the floor. It happened so fast he couldn't think. But his heart pounded and his brain was instantly awake. It could only be one thing. He reached up and switched off the lamp, then crawled away from the window to a side wall, then across the floor to the door. Reaching high again, he turned the knob, pulled open the door and crawled on all fours into the inn's upstairs hallway.

At Stu's room next door he pounded on the door. "Stu, get up! Answer the door, dammit."

There was no sound.

"Come on, Stu. Wake up. Dammit! Someone took a shot at me."

Nothing.

Brad waited and listened. The room was dead silent. So he turned and ran down the narrow hall in his underwear to the stairwell, and then down to the lobby. In the stillness of the night, worried about attracting a second shot through some other window, he cringed at each loud creak of the risers. The night manager was dozing in a small office just off the lobby, but awoke with the vibration of Brad's steps on the bouncy floor.

"I think someone took a shot at me just now," Brad said. "And my friend in the next room doesn't answer his door."

"Slow down," the manager said. "Did you see who did it? Is he still in the building?"

"No. Outside – through the window. Somewhere out front toward the water. The mirror exploded on the dresser behind me."

The manager reached into his drawer and pulled out a snub-nosed .38, clicked the magazine into place and set the gun on the desk. "For emergencies," he said. Then he dialed 911. "This is the Captain Whidbey front desk. We need the sheriff right now. One of our guests says someone took a shot at him through the window just now."

He paused and listened. "Captain Whidbey," he yelled into the phone. "There's only one. You don't need my damn address."

Another pause. "No, I'm not staying on the line. We're under attack here. I've got things to do."

Then the manager grabbed his master keys and led Brad upstairs again, to unlock Stu's room. Brad was already worried about what they might find.

But by the time they reached the upstairs hall, Stu was standing in the open doorway, fully dressed. He shrugged his shoulders, holding both arms with palms up in apparent confusion.

"What the heck is this?" Stu asked. "Aren't you supposed to be sleeping?"

"That's what I was going to ask you," Brad replied.

"Well I *couldn't* sleep," Stu said. "I've been out walking to unwind. This is a peaceful hour when the world is asleep, present company excepted."

"Did you hear anything out there?" Brad asked. "Like a gun with a silencer?"

"Are you serious?" Stu asked.

"Someone took a shot at me through the window."

"Holy crap. I didn't hear anything," Stu said, "but it was creepy out there. I had this odd feeling the whole time that I wasn't alone."

Stu's answer struck Brad as a little too convenient. The trio made their way down to the front desk as Shane Lindstrom, of all people, came through the lobby door with his gun drawn.

"I did a sweep of the grounds on my way in," he declared to the manager. "No sign of anyone. Did you check the beach for boats?" Turning to Brad and Stu he asked, "Are you the victims?"

"So it would seem," Brad said. "What are you doing here, and how did you get here so fast?"

"I'm on nights this week," Shane said. "I was headed south on the highway, just past the turnoff to Madrona Way, when I got the 911 dispatch. The sheriff is en route from Freeland. What happened here anyway?"

Outside, more vehicles were pulling up – Coupeville Town Marshall, Oak Harbor Police and a Whidbey General Hospital ambulance. Flashing red-and-blue lights lit up the parking lot and reflected off the trees and buildings.

"What is all this?" Brad asked.

"Mutual assistance," Shane explained. "We are spread paper thin in Island County so in any emergency, the jurisdictions back each other up. Now tell me again, what happened here?"

"I was up early, working by my window, when the mirror exploded behind me. It had to be a bullet."

"You sure?"

"What else would make a mirror explode?" Brad asked. "All I can say is thank God he missed."

"Maybe the shooter didn't miss," Shane said.

"How do you figure that?"

"Maybe the shot wasn't supposed to hit you. And have you considered the shooter might have been female?"

"Not in my wildest dreams," Brad said.

"Well let's not rule that out till we know."

"Either way I nearly got killed," Brad said. "If it was a message, I get it loud and clear. I've never been that close to a bullet before – a bullet in the head. I still can't stop shaking," he said.

"Did you piss off someone since the last time we talked?" Shane asked.

"Only the gentle shepherd, Father Benedict, as far as I know. But I let Stu handle that interview. He's good at it."

"Then we need to talk," Shane said. "After we look at that mirror.

Chapter 32

Doubts

Wood splinters fell to the glass-strewn dresser top as Shane dug the bullet out of the mirror's backing with a jackknife and tweezers. "Looks like about 9 mm, which is pretty common," he said. "Maybe from a Glock or some other small handgun fairly easy to conceal and carry."

Brad stared at the hole. "Even with a suppressor, I don't understand why nobody heard the shot. Silencers aren't that silent."

Shane held the slug in front of his face for a closer look before dropping it into a plastic bag. "You'd be surprised. Most of the noise with a suppressed handgun comes from the supersonic ammunition breaking the sound barrier. To get around that you use subsonic ammo. It's much quieter."

Stu wrinkled his brow and turned to Brad. "This whole thing is getting pretty serious. It may be time to think about getting back on the airplane and letting the sheriff sort it out."

Brad didn't like the thoughts that were going through his mind. Stu was his friend and now Brad wasn't sure he could trust him anymore. Stu had been reluctant to come to Bella's memorial and reluctant to get involved in investigating her death. By some improbable coincidence he had flown here the weekend of Bella's death and hadn't owned up until Brad pressed him.

It troubled Brad that Stu might be sick with terminal cancer, but troubled him even more that it might be a lie. Stu was not in his room at 4-something a.m. when someone took a shot at Brad, and Stu had no witness to corroborate where he was. Stu was doing all he could to deflect suspicion toward Father Benedict. Now he was suggesting the two of them go back to Idaho before they got to the bottom of it.

In an odd way Brad could never explain, some part of Stu had always seemed unknowable, as if there were some dark place within him he couldn't or wouldn't share. His recent secrecy and inconsistent behavior only added to that impression. Now after all these decades, it seemed both Bella and Stu were greater mysteries to Brad than ever.

And for the first time, Brad found himself thinking back on Amy's car accident and wondering if an overworked and understaffed county sheriff in the boondocks of Idaho might have missed what really happened on that mountain road.

"So what do you think?" Stu asked, jolting Brad back from his thoughts.

"About what?"

"Maybe it's time we bow graciously out of here and let the guys with guns and badges handle the rest."

"Not a chance," Brad said. "I am so damned pissed. You're free to go if you want, but this has gotten very personal. I'm not going anywhere till I know who killed Bella, and who took a shot at me."

Chapter 33

Touching Base

Brad sat alone on the patio of the Captain Whidbey, nursing a Corona and staring at a sailboat riding the afternoon breeze. Just across the choppy waters he could make out the historic, one-room schoolhouse at San de Fuca, where generations of youngsters no doubt passed crushingly normal days, as all kids do, daydreaming out the window.

He wasn't sure what he would say to Irene. Things weren't normal at home and certainly not here on Whidbey. He had come here to find closure to a lifetime of unfinished business with Bella, hoping that by laying her memory to rest, and their history, he might somehow be able to pick up the pieces with Irene.

Instead Bella was more at the center of his thoughts than ever. From the evidence on her computer she had never stopped thinking of him – in the move to this island, the dog she adopted, the web searches and the cryptic last email.

His friend Stu apparently was seriously ill, but could be covering up some unfinished business of his own with Bella. Her own priest and the policeman next door were either her last trusted friends or betrayers who had hastened her death.

Then there was the small matter that someone had taken a shot at him. How do you bring that up in passing?

Brad and Irene hadn't talked for several days since he and Stu flew to the island – just exchanged texts to say everything was ok. In the unwritten rules of marriage, he was pretty sure he owed her a phone call about nearly getting shot. He just didn't want to upset her.

He pulled the phone from his pocket, stared at Irene's name, then punched the button. She picked up before it even rang.

"Hi Brad," she answered.

"Hi honey. How are things there?"

"Sitting on the porch with Bear, watching the clouds roll by."

"Give him a little ear massage for me, will you? How are you getting along?" he asked.

"We're doing famously. Yourself?"

Brad heard a resonant thunk over the line. He knew the sound – a cork popping. "Just a sec," Irene said. Apparently she needed a little anesthetic to get her through this conversation.

You would think a writer would have all the right words. But when it came to Irene, Brad couldn't write or talk his way out of paper bag.

"Ok, I'm back."

"Happy hour?"

"How did you guess?"

"Things here are complicated," Brad said. "I hoped we might be headed home by now but we're in the middle of a mess. Somebody murdered Bella."

"I'm sorry," Irene said. "But I thought she took her own life. Are the police investigating?"

"Kinda. But it's complicated. I don't know if we can trust them. Stu hates the priest and his instincts might be right. Stu is also ready to leave. And he says he has leukemia."

"Oh my god, no," Irene said. "How long does he have?"

"I don't know. He isn't saying much. I don't even know if he's leveling with me about that. And there's something else."

"Yeah?"

"Someone took a shot at me through the window this morning."

"What?"

"I'm fine. The window's broken. My new buddy the sheriff's detective thinks it was a warning not intended to hit me."

"Listen," Brad said. "I know I've made a mess of things between us. I want to try harder to be a better husband. When I get back, I think we should do some counseling together. But I just need a little more time here."

"We had a good life once," Irene said.

"I don't see why we can't have it again."

"I'm not sure. Things are different. Amy's gone. Stu may be gone soon. In a way you left a long time ago. I'm not sure we belong together."

"Let's take it one step at a time," Brad said. "It takes a while to unravel these things."

"No promises."

"I can't ask you to. When I leave here I'll be driving a rental car. I'm bringing home another member of the family."

"Exactly what does that mean?"

"Ida – short for Idaho. Bella had a dog and she's now homeless. A really sweet girl. She needs a farm and some love for her remaining years. Bear might like a girlfriend."

Chapter 34

Witness

"Somebody saw us," Benedict said. "Absolutely no question. I heard it and so did you."

"It won't come to anything," Dutch DeGroot said, removing his glasses and rubbing his eyes. "He apparently took off running when we turned and looked. It was just some kid getting his jollies watching two old queers who mean nothing to him."

"A lot of kids know me," Benedict said. "If it was someone who knows me and this gets back to his parents or school . . ."

"It could be someone from North Dakota camping in the park overnight."

"Or someone from my church," Benedict said.

Chapter 35

Another Floater

The body was fresh.

"In the water maybe 12 hours," remarked Island County Coroner Garth Higgenbotham as he waded up to his knees and took hold of the floating arms of the body. "And pretty beat up. He hit the water hard."

Half-a-dozen onlookers stood on the rocky shore of the west side of Ben Ure Island, just at the entrance of Cornet Bay, where Deception Pass State Park maintains a rental cabin for guests who want to leave civilization behind, but not too far. Guests in the cabin often have the entire island to themselves, but are just a five-minute rowboat ride from the busiest park in the state park system.

Park ranger Don Adams nodded. "We had a big tide flowing in through the pass during the night. If he jumped after midnight, the tide probably carried him straight here on the current."

Higgenbotham turned to the group and his eyes settled on a young couple in shorts and T-shirts toward the back. "And you folks found him, I take it?"

"Yeah," the man said. "Just like that, face down, right after first light. He was pretty well lodged in the kelp. First we thought he was maybe a dead harbor seal because they haul out all over here on the rocks. Once we realized he wasn't, we didn't want to touch him, so we called the park office on my cell and then stayed here to make sure the body didn't float anywhere."

Shane Lindstrom cut in. "You're staying in the park's cabin?"

"Yeah we were out for a morning hike around the island. We are booked for one more night in the cabin but after this I'm not sure," he said, looking at the pony-tailed woman beside him and raising his eyebrows. "This isn't the memory we had in mind for this week."

"Before you go anywhere I'll need you to fill out a complete written statement."

Higgenbotham, joined by Adams, pulled the body up on the beach and turned it over.

"Hey, I know that guy," Shane said. "I want you to go over him very carefully because he's a suspect in an investigation. If there's anything suspicious about the way he died, I've got to know."

Chapter 36

Confession

A late-morning knock on Brad's door at The Captain Whidbey roused him from a senior citizen nap. Growing old is pathetic, Brad thought. You can't sleep at night and can't stay awake during the day.

He sat up on the edge of the bed, groggy, rubbing the sides of his head, and grunted, "Coming. Hang on."

It was Shane Lindstrom.

"Let's get your friend Stu over here so the three of us can discus something," Shane suggested. Brad wasn't sure if Shane was thinking out loud or giving him an order, but he stepped out into the hall in his rumpled T-shirt and jeans and knocked on Stu's door. When Stu finally answered, Brad couldn't help noticing Stu was unkempt and bleary eyed, as if he hadn't slept much either. Brad gestured for Shane and Stu to sit in the room's two arm chairs. Brad pulled wrinkles out of his bedspread and sat down on the edge of the mattress. When they were all seated, Shane began.

"We have a confession to Bella's murder," he said, nodding toward Brad."

Brad leaned forward. Stu squinted and cocked his head.

Shane let the suspense sit for a moment while he looked straight at Stu, then Brad, then declared: "Father Benedict."

"No shit!" Stu responded, pounding his fist into the palm of his other hand. "So he's talking?"

"Not really," Shane said. "He wrote it out. We pulled him from the water this morning."

"What water?"

"Deception Pass," Shane responded.

Brad grimaced. "Did he jump or was he pushed?"

"You tell me," Shane said. "We don't know how he got to the bridge. His car was back at the church, and a note explaining everything was sitting in the tray of his printer."

"That's more than Bella left," Brad interjected.

"No, she didn't have luxury of leaving us any last words," Shane agreed. "Benedict didn't sign the note but it was a very detailed, comprehensive account of Bella's murder and the reasons."

"And . . . ?" Brad asked.

"And I won't go into all the specifics since this is an active investigation, but the gist is that he confessed to killing Bella, felt remorse and wanted to atone. In his mind jumping seemed the only right way to do that."

Stu scowled. "Coward."

"If," Brad interjected, "he's even the person who killed Bella."

"C'mon, you know it was him," Stu objected. "Whether he jumped or was pushed, he got what he had coming. And for crying out loud he took a shot at you, too."

Brad interrupted. "How do we know he's the one who shot at me? Was that in his note?"

"No," Shane said. "Nothing about that."

"I think we're pretty sure he sexually abused some young boys in the church," Brad said, "though we have no proof. It seems clear Bella discovered this or strongly suspected it. But that doesn't prove Benedict killed her, or even that the threat of exposure was the issue."

"Yes it does," Stu said, "because Shane has his note confessing to it. I'd lay odds one of his victims was Billy Sizemore. I've seen kids like him before after a pedophile has gotten hold of them. And if Benedict isn't the one who killed Bella, then who do *you* think it was?"

Brad rested his chin on his hand and stared into space.

"Benedict's suicide feels a little too neat and tidy," he said, "just like Bella's."

Chapter 37

Face to Face

Dorothy DeGroot couldn't believe her good fortune. Events had taken a turn she'd never foreseen with Benedict's suicide and the note he left behind. The sheriff had shared it with her. What motive Benedict had in writing that note, DeGroot couldn't fathom. Was it a parting gift to her husband? She had suspected for some time that Dutch was having a relationship with the priest. Her marriage to Dutch had been strictly a platonic financial and political arrangement for years.

Benedict's death tied up some loose ends and lifted a heavy weight from the commissioner. She was in a good mood when her receptionist paged her for the first appointment of the day.

"My goodness, this is an honor and pleasure," Dorothy DeGroot said as she pumped Brad's arm, grinning broadly and guiding him with her free arm to a chair on the other side of the desk.

"You're the Garrison Keillor of Idaho," DeGroot declared.

"There's only one Garrison Keillor," Brad replied. "I just write stories, best I can."

"I've heard you on National Public Radio. What brings you to Coupeville of all places?"

"Well I'm looking into an old friend's murder," Brad explained. "Bella Morelli and I were classmates in journalism at the university."

"That's going back a long time," DeGroot said. "Morelli . . . Morelli," she repeated, wrinkling her brow and staring up at the ceiling as if concentrating hard to place the name.

"She was found dead under Deception Pass Bridge a few weeks ago," Brad offered to nudge DeGroot's memory.

"Ok yes, coming back to me – I read the story in the paper. A sad story on top of another sad story. It's just a horrible tragedy that whatever happened between Bella and Father Benedict, it ended up causing the padre to take his own life as well."

"I wondered if you ever met Bella," Brad asked, poker faced.

"Boy, I can't say that I recall."

". . . Because she was pretty high profile in the Growler controversy."

"Well . . . now that you refresh my memory, I did see some letters about her in the newspaper. We hear so much about that from so many that it all runs together after while. But yes, I think she touched a nerve with some."

Brad continued, "She left some notes indicating she interviewed you. And with your real estate holdings, I expect she would have been a burr under your saddle as well."

"Well, Mr. Haraldsen, I believe she did! One thing I've learned in public life is not to take anything personally. Most people mean well. They don't always agree but they mean well, and it's my job to listen and get along with them all, and try to bring the opposing sides together."

"You're a Catholic, aren't you?" Brad asked. "That was Ms. Morelli's religion."

"No, we Dutch are all Christian Reformed but people sometimes think I'm Catholic – if you can believe it with a name like mine. I maintain good relationships across the faith community," DeGroot said.

"So you knew Father Benedict?"

"Professionally," DeGroot said. "Brilliant man and a great asset to the community, rest his soul. I still can't fathom what caused him to kill Bella and then take his own life, too, but his guilt must have been unbearable. What a terrible loss and a terrible waste of both their lives."

"Your development company has made donations to Benedict's church, I believe," Brad said.

"It's possible. I don't micromanage it – that's more Dutch's area. But we try to encourage and reward worthy enterprises like Our Lady of the Cove and the work of Father Benedict. This community is going to miss him."

"I got the impression from Bella's notes that you were perhaps more than just casually involved with that church," Brad said.

"I'm not sure what might have been in any notes you're referring to."

"Well, she left quite a trail that we've found," Brad said.

"My gosh," DeGroot said. "I hope whatever she left, it ties up any loose ends. The facts sure seem straightforward and sad."

"Just the opposite, Mrs. DeGroot. The facts are more confusing than ever."

"Well if there is anything I can do to help, don't hesitate to ask," DeGroot offered, scooting back her chair and standing – a signal to Brad that the meeting was over.

Chapter 38

Open and Shut

"I'll walk you back to your car," Brad volunteered to Shane at the end of their meeting. When they reached the parking lot, away from watchful eyes and ears, Brad whispered, "Dorothy DeGroot is hiding something."

"Why do you say that?"

"I talked with her at the courthouse. She acted like she didn't know Bella – couldn't even place the name till I refreshed her memory. Then she downplayed how well she knew Benedict. I took the opportunity to shake her up by saying Bella left quite a trail of notes, and I think she's rattled now."

"Nevertheless," Shane replied, "we have Benedict's note explaining both deaths – his own and Bella's. We have motive, means and opportunity, and a confession."

"What about the confession? Are you going to release it to the newspaper?"

"No, the sheriff has agreed to withhold it while I look into the circumstances of his death."

"Do we have the gun, the one he used to shoot at me?" Brad asked.

"No we don't and that bothers me. I'm looking."

"I guess your boss and *his* boss, Dot DeGroot, wouldn't mind if the whole investigation ends here."

Shane kept a straight face. "It's our job to close cases."

"Are you personally going to drop this now?" Brad asked.

"As far as the department is concerned, yes," Shane replied. "As far as I'm concerned personally as Bella's friend, it doesn't feel finished. Bella got into something big enough that I think she disturbed a nest of snakes. I think that's what this is about."

"More than pedophilia?"

"That's my gut," Shane said. "I didn't buy Bella's death as a suicide. Neither could I see Benedict as a murderer, and I sure don't see him as a suicide. He was too wily and smart, too much of a fighter and survivor with the past he's had and everything he built here in Coupeville. Like you, I feel an obligation to Bella as a friend to try to find out what happened."

"I found the beginnings of a story in Bella's computer files," Brad said. "She was digging into the DeGroots real estate empire and their cozy relationship with the Navy."

"Dot DeGroot is someone you don't want to cross. Money and politics, and power, go together. DeGroot has held a tight grip on all three for a long time. As county commissioner she has appointed her spies and friends to every committee. She's got people in every office and organization in the community."

"Including the Catholic church and the sheriff's department?"

"Absolutely."

"Any chance that includes Smokey Sizemore, the Navy pilot? Could he have been feeding information to DeGroot."

"It's the kind of thing Dot would do," Shane said. "If you take care of her, she takes care of you."

"But not you? You're the investigating officer. DeGroot hasn't asked you to keep her posted?"

"No. I'm sure my boss the sheriff is doing that."

"Were you more than a friend to Bella?" Brad asked.

"If you want to put it that way," Shane replied. "When the threats started coming, she leaned on me to protect her. I liked that role. The more I was with her, the more I admired her spirit. She also had a vulnerability that was very attractive to the man in me – that quality, the breathy voice. She got to me pretty deeply, maybe like she did you."

"But she was 67 years old and you're, what, mid-50s?"

"She was a young 67. I never thought about the age difference."

"Did this cause you some problems at home?"

"Wives have radar for this stuff. This job is hard enough on relationships as it is," Shane said, adding that when he took his rookie police training the instructor warned the cadets that good marriages are hard, and good police marriages even harder."

"Why do you think that is?" Brad asked.

"It's hard for a cop to be vulnerable," Shane said. "We're trained to suppress our feelings and take control of situations, not to admit when we're hurting emotionally."

Brad confessed he'd been struggling with that himself, being honest about his emotions, and he had nowhere near the pressure on him Shane did.

"Did your wife know how you felt about Bella?" Shane asked.

"I hadn't seen Bella in 30 years but I think Irene always knew she was second to Bella in my heart. Things aren't too good at home these days. I need to get back there and sort out what's next, but I'm not done with this," Brad said. "But speaking of Idaho, that's Bella's dog in your back seat, isn't it?"

"Yes," Shane said. "Would you like to have her? It rips my heart out when a dog gets passed around in a situation like this. I don't want to turn Ida over to the shelter. I'd rather send her home with you than give her to strangers."

"I'd like her," Brad said. "Could I take her in a few days when I leave? She's too big for Stu's airplane. When I get ready to leave I'll rent a car and drive back to Stanley with her. She's all that's left of Bella for me now. We'll take our time, stop a lot on the way, savor the journey."

"How are you and Stu doing at this point?"

"I don't know. The trust isn't what it was. Maybe it was never really there. I think there's something he isn't telling me."

"I do, too. Maybe you can figure it out over time and let me know."

Chapter 39

Surveillance Cam

Shane Lindstrom took a sip of coffee and turned back to the computer in his den. He'd been at this for three hours, watching a speeded-up video of cars entering and leaving Deception Pass State Park. He had selected the Friday evening before Bella's body was found, starting with the late afternoon and early evening hours.

It was tedious work after a day at the office, but he did not want questions about this from the sheriff till he knew more. He was watching primarily for just three vehicles – Bella's Prius, Father Benedict's Corolla and Dorothy DeGroot's Ford Expedition. Whenever the right make and model vehicle crossed his view, he slowed the video and studied it frame-by-frame.

There it was! The Prius.

A moment later, a second vehicle crossed his view and he was sure.

He picked up the phone and dialed.

"It's Shane," he said. "You know where I live. I think you'd better get over here right now and look at this."

*

Shane met Brad at the door and led him to the den.

"I've been reviewing some video," Shane said. "Don Adams, the head ranger at the park, installed a camera a couple of years ago and didn't say much about it. It's well concealed near the entrance station so he can keep an eye on vehicles entering the park that aren't displaying the required parks pass."

"Seriously?" Brad asked. "It's a state park, and they take video of their visitors?"

"The entrance station is only staffed during peak hours. Every so often Don gets an AmeriCorps volunteer who needs something to do, so he puts the kid to work an hour a day, reviewing video and compiling statistics to help justify Adams' requests for more staffing."

"Anyway, I asked Don for a jump drive of video for the period just before Bella's body was found."

"And?" Brad asked.

"At 8:27 that Friday evening, Bella's Prius entered the park. That's about 10 minutes before sunset. I ran her plate and confirmed it."

"That makes sense," Brad said. "We know the car was still there in the parking lot at North Beach after her body was found two days later."

"So take a look at this," Shane continued. "This is the DeGroots Ford Expedition entering the park at 8:35 that same evening."

"Holy cow," Brad exclaimed. "What about Benedict?"

"What about him? He's not on this video."

"Did the camera catch the DeGroots leaving the park?" Brad asked.

"9:07 pm. That's enough time to catch up with Bella on foot, walk her to the bridge, help her over the rail, and get back to the car and leave."

"My God."

"It doesn't prove anything but it's suspicious as all hell. I can't haul them in with just this or they'll deny everything but coincidence. It's a big park with lots of roads, campgrounds and beaches."

"Yes, but the noose is tightening," Brad said. "We just need a little more."

Chapter 40

Tidying Up

Standing alone at the end of Coupeville Wharf, as night gave way to the first suggestion of sunrise, Stu reached into his pocket and dropped something heavy into the water with a loud plop. A few bubbles rose from the inky blackness as it sank. At low tide he knew the water here was only a few feet deep, but it was deep enough to float boats and the bottom was muddy. He hoped it was muddy enough to erase this from his life.

Brad was giving him a lift to the Oak Harbor airfield later this morning, and would stay a few more days before driving back to Idaho with Bella's dog.

By then, Stu would finish what he had to do.

Chapter 41

Clearing the Air

Brad had a bad feeling that Stu was in a hurry to leave. If they didn't talk this morning, he wasn't sure when they would.

"Can we take a few minutes before you go?" Brad asked. "I feel like we're leaving things at a bad place between us."

Brad drove to Ebey's Landing, and they got out and made their way to a big, bleached drift log. The morning air was fresh, the beach was deserted, and the sun was at their backs, casting a golden glow on the sand and logs. Red-winged Blackbirds sang in the reeds.

"This place reminds me of Bella," Brad said, "knowing she liked to walk here. I can see why."

"What's on your mind, Brad?" Stu asked, glancing at his watch.

"I'm thinking we've had a lot of losses, you and me," Brad began. "We're getting older. You lost Amy. I seem to be losing Irene. We've both lost Bella, and now you're sick. This getting old is a rough ride."

"It happens."

"Bella told me a story once about a priest and a little boy, but never said who the boy was. I think it affected her pretty deeply," Brad said.

"Yeah?"

"Did she ever share it with you?"

"No."

"I think the boy was you," Brad said.

Stu stared at the water. Seconds passed. "I never told anyone," he said. "Just Bella. She promised she would keep it a secret."

"She did – never revealed your name."

"And," Brad continued, "maybe this had something to do with your opinion of Benedict."

"He was a fraud. I could smell it. He got what he deserved and Bella got justice. That's why we came here, right, to even the score?"

"Are you sure he killed her?"

"Pretty sure. And even if he didn't, he was a pedophile and was ruining people's lives, and Bella found out, and it's probably why she ended up under the bridge."

"So who do you think killed Benedict?"

"Maybe the guilt just got to him – maybe he killed himself."

"Or," Brad said, "maybe someone helped him over the rail."

"Possibly. A good Samaritan."

"If they did, how did they get him to go along with it?"

"Maybe the person was packing a persuader, to help him make the right decision."

"Speaking of guns, did you take a shot at me the other morning?"

"Wow," Stu said. "I can't believe you just blurt that out. If I did, I would have made sure to miss."

Without a word, Brad turned and swung his fist at Stu, hitting him in the side of the head and knocking him into a tangle of logs on his hands and knees. A cut opened up by Stu's ear.

"Jeesus, Brad, what the hell was that? I'm bleeding like a stuck pig."

Stu fished a handkerchief from his back pocket and held it to his head.

"Do you have *any* idea what you did?" Brad asked. "You could have killed me."

"You're always so damn cautious," Stu said. "All the way back to college you always played it safe. We had Benedict dead to rights and you weren't taking him seriously. I had to do something to wake you up and get you mad enough to go after him. You needed a push to see the obvious."

"So you just figured it was worth the small risk the bullet might not go where you aimed?"

"I'm a pretty good shot. I made sure to aim way wide and high."

Do you still have the gun?"

"The gun is someplace it will never be found. By the way, how did Irene take it when you told her about the gunshot."

"Not too well. Bullets flying is a little more than she what she thought this trip was about."

"She still cares about you," Stu said. "I hope you'll go home when this is over and try again with her. You had something good. You can get it back again."

"I'm going to try," Brad said. "But about this other business – you taking a shot at me – you know I have to tell Shane."

"Yeah," Stu said, "I know. Just give me a few minutes to get off the ground and then do whatever you need to do."

"Why throw everything away like this? Best you can hope for now is to spend the rest of your life behind bars."

"My life is over," Stu said. "Leukemia," he reminded Brad. "It's amazing how freeing that is. The only question is when, and how much I want to suffer and drag it out. Since I know how the story ends I can afford to fuss with the timing and expedite justice with Father Benedict. And as long as I've got that airplane, I can go out on my own terms."

"So your trip to Snohomish the weekend of Bella's death had nothing to do with her?"

"Absolutely nothing. Hell of a coincidence. Shane must be doing back flips over it."

"I'm sorry about the leukemia," Brad said. "I wanted things to be so different – for us to grow old together in the mountains, doing what we love."

"We did ok," Stu said. "We stuck together – you and me and Bella – even when we were apart. Rooming with you at the university is still the best thing that ever happened to me. No one is perfect. We all have secrets, but now you know mine. We all do things we'd like to take back. To err is human."

*

They drove in silence to Eisenberg Airfield near Monroe Landing. Brad waited while Stu went over the airplane, checking it carefully.

"Not sure why I'm doing this," Stu muttered at one point. "Habit."

When he was all finished, Stu came over and shook Brad's hand. "I'm sorry about the gun," Stu said.

"I'm sorry about slugging you but I'd probably do it again," Brad replied. Then he wrapped his arms around Stu and hugged him tightly.

"See you on the other side," Stu said. He climbed up on the wing, lowered himself into the cockpit, pulled down the canopy and pushed the starter. A blast of prop wash swept over Brad and whipped at his hair and shirt as Stu tested the rudder and flaps. Then he turned and taxied across the grass to the pavement.

Brad watched Stu roll smartly to the far end of the strip, turn and stop, rev up the RPMs, then release the brakes. The engine roared as the aircraft closed rapidly on Brad, lifted clear and passed low over the hangars. Stu, in his white cowboy hat, waved from the cockpit.

He circled west, then banked east toward the Cascade Mountains and climbed till all that remained was a tiny dot among the clouds. It grew smaller and smaller, till Brad could find it no more.

Chapter 42

Tightening the Net

Brad called Shane and went over what he'd learned.

"I don't think we'll see him again," Brad said. "He has no intention of ever arriving at his destination. Now there's just the unresolved question of who killed Bella, which was where this whole thing started."

Shane revealed there had been one small break – a report of lewd behavior a few evenings ago at Goose Rock. The witness was the son of a liberal town councilman from Coupeville, a vocal opponent of the Growler. He told his dad he recognized the men involved – Father Benedict and Dutch DeGroot.

"That's political dynamite," Brad said. "It doesn't prove either of the DeGroots had anything to do with Bella's death but does give Dutch and Benedict a motive to be plenty nervous about Bella. Then again, in light of town councilman's obvious interest in discrediting the DeGroots, they could dismiss it as sheer mudslinging by someone with a political agenda."

"It's something I can use to make Dot squirm when I get ready to talk to her," Shane said.

"We also have the draft on Bella's computer of her story about Dot and the Growler, which was quite unfavorable, and we know Dot lied to me about the extent of her contacts with both Bella and Benedict. And the video of her entering the park a few minutes after Bella before she disappeared."

Brad paused a moment, then continued. "Did Benedict leave a cell phone, maybe a history of texts to DeGroot?"

"It must have gone over the rail with him. There's no sign of it. If it's on the bottom, I guarantee you no one's going after it."

"Computer?"

"Just church stuff. The church had a Facebook page, which he maintained. No trail of email to Dutch or Dot, nor to Bella. Dot was more of a pick-up-the-phone gal, people said, kind of old school."

As they were talking, Brad grasped at straws. He went back over what he and Stu already had learned.

"Maybe Stu left us a parting gift," Brad said. He shared with Shane what Stu had said about his conversation with Fawn Sizemore. Fawn had told Stu that her husband and a friend named "A.J." were gun enthusiasts and went shooting together. She didn't care for the guy — called him a right-wing nut.

Someone named "A.J. Ludke, American patriot" had written hostile letters to the newspaper about Bella. Shane told Brad someone had blown up Bella's mailbox a few days before she was killed.

"Maybe it's time you squeeze A.J. a little," Brad suggested. "Can I go along for the ride?"

"Yes, but first I need your help with a little grunt work."

Chapter 43

Beachcombing

Brad and Shane started their search in the parking lot at North Beach. "This is a long shot," Shane said, "but it's how cases are built. We need a break. If we don't look, we might overlook the one piece of evidence that could break this open."

The two combed the parking lot systematically for anything that could have rolled off a car seat or been dropped absentmindedly, focusing closely on the spot where Bella's car had sat for two days. What they found were candy wrappers, plastic bags, French fries, chewing gum, Styrofoam cups, Coke cans, one tampon, a shopping list and vomit.

"The vomit is interesting," Shane said. "If you had just killed someone, might you have been sick to your stomach?"

"Maybe," Brad said, "but people get sick from eating this other stuff. I'm not picking it up. We've got nothing."

"Well, it's probably too fresh – doesn't last long in the rain – but I'd never forgive myself if I left some DNA that I wished I had later," Shane said, scooping a sample of it into a clean plastic bag."

"Is that all you need for today?" Brad asked.

"We're not done yet."

They followed the trail down to the water's edge, studying the ground and bushes every step of the way. At the beach, Shane gave Brad the bad news.

"Now it gets harder, because we don't know where Bella might have been sitting when the DeGroots caught up with her, assuming that's how it happened. So we just have to go over every inch of this beach and woody debris, looking for anything we can link to them."

The beach was a mess – plastic monofilament line, foam insulation, fried chicken bones, several boards, an unopened package of Mike 'n Ike sour candy, crab shells, a dead Pigeon Guillemot and some nylon rope, everything half covered with sand.

"Somebody has good taste," Brad declared, holding up a piece of foil.

Shane looked up. "Give me that," he said. "Now we are getting somewhere."

Chapter 44

Missing

Brad couldn't get Stu out of his mind all day. He hoped Stu had changed his mind somewhere over the Cascade Mountains, but in his heart he knew it was not likely. As he drove back to the Captain Whidbey that evening, a bulletin on the radio confirmed it.

KUOW has learned that a single-engine aircraft that left Whidbey Island this morning is missing over the Cascade Mountains. Chelan County Sheriff's Deputies are combing an area of Lake Chelan south of Stehekin for debris from an airplane that plunged into water this morning. Eyewitnesses said the aircraft struck at a steep angle and disintegrated and sank on impact. The lake is one of the deepest fjords in North America and recovery of the aircraft and any human remains may be difficult. If it is the missing aircraft, the pilot, a resident of Idaho, is believed to be the only person aboard.

And so it goes, a lifetime reduced to a few well-crafted words delivered in a baritone voice on a drive-time newscast.

Stu had gone out on his own terms, gone "home" in a sense to where he grew up. Brad couldn't fault him for that but regretted Stu would not be around to see justice for Bella. He and Shane were building a box around the DeGroots, Brad believed. Whether they could keep them inside it, he wasn't sure. Dot DeGroot was enormously popular for her charm and her outspoken support of the Navy.

"I'm way out on a limb with this DeGroot business," Shane said. "If we can't pin Bella's murder on them I'm finished in this county. Dot covers her tracks well and has plenty of friends in high places, all the way up to the Pentagon."

"And including your boss, the sheriff," Brad remarked.

"Specifically him. For our department she is the goose that laid the golden egg. When the commissioners set the county budget, DeGroot makes sure we get everything we want. My boss will be the last to undermine or embarrass them in any way.

"On the other hand," he continued, "if the golden goose broke the law and we can prove it, the sheriff isn't going to line up on the losing side. He'll cut his losses. If he can bring down the biggest crooks in Island County history, he'll take the credit for that and come out even stronger."

"So now what?" Brad asked.

"We nibble around the edges."

Chapter 45

American Patriot

- *No Trespassing.*

- *Survivors Will Be Prosecuted.*

- *Insured by Smith and Wesson.*

The hand-painted signs were spaced like an old Burma Shave promotion along the narrow driveway leading into the woods. The road led to a clearing where a rusting truck and a decomposing travel trailer decorated the view.

- *Home of the Brave.*

- *Land of the Free.*

Those were the last two.

A.J. Ludke, apparently a bachelor, lived on five acres of woods near Strawberry Point, northeast of Oak Harbor, in a kit home with peeling paint and dry rot. At least Brad assumed Ludke was a bachelor, since he could not picture any woman who would live like this. Tall, unmowed grass surrounded the home. By a shed Brad noted a stack of fresh, fragrant firewood and a Stihl chainsaw. A four-wheel-drive Ford F-250 sat out front. *Guns, God and Guts* was plastered across the back bumper. A rifle rack filled the rear window.

"I'm getting a picture of the man before we even get out of the car," Brad said.

They could hear the news channel blaring from the TV as soon as they opened the doors of Shane's patrol car.

Shane knocked. "Mr. Ludke," he called loudly. "It's Shane Lindstrom, Island County Sheriff's Department."

Inside the home, barking erupted. The TV must have masked their approach from the dog.

"Hang on," came the reply. "Let me get this dog under control." The TV went dead.

The door opened to a wiry man, about 40, maybe 5-8, with thick black hair and plastic horn-rims riding atop anvil-type sideburns, dressed in torn jeans and a faded flannel shirt covered with sawdust. He smelled of chainsaw oil and exhaust.

"I've been bucking firewood," he explained.

Shane planted his shoulder with the US flag toward Ludke. Brad thought it a nice touch. "This is Brad Haraldsen," Shane began, "a member of my citizens patrol." Brad was impressed. He was official now.

Behind Ludke on a table in the living room, Brad could see a reloading press. There'd be some black powder in this place, the makings of a good, homemade stick of dynamite. Brad also could see a few beer bottles, and a house that hadn't been cleaned in a while.

"What can I do for you?" Ludke asked, standing his ground in the open doorway.

"We're following up leads in the death of woman from Admiral's Cove a couple of weeks ago."

"Does this have something to do with me?" Ludke asked.

"No, no," Shane said. "But you may have known her and some others who knew her. We're trying to build a picture of her last few days. The name is Bella Morelli."

"Am I a suspect or something?"

"Not at all. But I'd appreciate your help. If you help me, I'll keep that in mind if our investigation leads toward any associates of yours."

"Bella Morelli was a well known liberal and a Muslim, prominently anti-Navy," Ludke said. "I'm not sorry she's no longer with us."

"She was a friend of mine," Brad piped up.

"You should choose your friends more carefully," Ludke replied. "By the way this is private property."

"This is just a friendly discussion," Shane said. "I prefer friendly rather than dragging a judge or prosecutor into things. If you'll indulge me, I believe you wrote some letters to the newspaper about Ms. Morelli," Shane continued.

"That's true."

"And a truck like yours was seen leaving her neighborhood at the time someone dynamited her mailbox a while back."

"Well I hope my truck didn't break any laws. People borrow my truck and I don't always know where it goes."

"You should choose your friends more carefully," Brad interjected. Shane turned and scowled at Brad, and drew his hand across his neck in the universal sign for "cut," while Ludke was looking down.

"Do you know a Navy pilot named Smokey Sizemore?" Shane continued.

"Yeah I met him at the range a while back. We go shooting sometimes."

"Did the subject of Bella come up between you?"

"We talk about a lot of things. We probably talked about her, since she was so anti-Navy."

"Did you talk about encouraging her to leave the island?"

"We both thought she could use some encouragement."

"How about Dorothy DeGroot? Do you know her?"

"Everyone knows her."

"Do you talk to her?"

"Yeah, I stop to see her in her office sometimes. We talk."

"About what?"

"She values my opinion. The Navy. We are on the same page about that."

"Well I hear you. If we lose the Navy this community will be nothing. On that issue I'd say you are what media experts call an *opinion leader*," Shane said.

"I know the term and it's a fair statement," Ludke said, smiling. "I choose to be an informed citizen. I communicate with our elected representatives and you probably see my name on the editorial pages. That's how democracy works."

"I understand Dot encouraged you to write those letters to the newspaper about Ms. Morelli."

Wow! Brad knew this was a shot in the dark and a bold one. Shane phrased it as a statement of fact, not a question. Ludke hesitated, no doubt realizing Shane had backed him into a corner. Ludke couldn't be sure whether Shane already knew this from DeGroot or not. If he denied DeGroot had put him up to writing the letters, he could be caught in a lie. If he confirmed it, he might be giving Shane information he did not yet have.

Ludke thought a moment. "Yes, that was Dot's idea. I can write a decent letter and be a little more direct, shall we say, than she can as a county commissioner."

"You seem like a stand-up guy," Shane observed. "If I could take you into my confidence for a moment, since you know Dot pretty well, let me ask if you ever noticed something a little bit off about her husband."

"Off? Like what?"

"I want to be diplomatic here and *don't* want to make something out of nothing. There were rumors, you know, about Dutch and Father Benedict."

"Rumors?"

"Deviant sexual behavior. It's their private business, of course, as long as it stays between consenting adults. But it's not the America I grew up in. Some people think Dutch DeGroot is a little effeminate. I'm just curious if it came back in some way against Ms. Morelli. It appears she saw or suspected Benedict did something inappropriate involving children in the church. He and Dutch may have had their own reasons for wanting her out of community beyond the Growler. I wondered if you'd seen anything or had any unsettling questions about Dutch or his wife."

"Good god, what? What was that Morelli writing?"

"Pretty explosive stuff. Did Smokey ever mention any concerns about his children and Father Benedict?"

"What kind of concerns?"

"Billy Sizemore has been pretty moody and quiet for the last year. We had a report that Billy observed Bella and Father Benedict arguing, and that he did not want to see Bella hurt any more. One theory is that Father Benedict may have been grooming him."

Brad was astounded. Shane had linked the DeGroots to Benedict and driven a wedge between Dutch and Ludke and Sizemore. He had invoked a bit of flattery, some patriotism, some homophobia, and sown doubts that could isolate the commissioner. Ludke would be on the phone to Sizemore within minutes, he was sure.

"Well," Shane finished up, "I'd appreciate a call if you remember anything more," handing Ludke his card. "You've been a big help."

Back at the car, Brad turned to Shane. "Nicely done. Nobody wants to be a big help to the police when they're involved in something shady."

"I'm operating without a net," Shane said. "Let's just hope he doesn't call DeGroot. If he does, this could come back to bite me fast in a very big way."

Chapter 46

Smokey

They didn't wait long. Brad and Shane had just sat down to lunch of carnitas de pollo at La Marimba Mexican Restaurant in Oak Harbor's Old Town when Shane received a page from his dispatcher.

"Sorry to bother you but Captain Smokey Sizemore asks you to call him. Says it's important."

"Will do," Shane replied. He took a bite of onions and beans from his plate and turned to Brad. "This is heavenly. Take a bite. I've got to make this call because we're getting to the fun part now."

Smokey, it turned out, had just gotten off the phone with his shooting buddy, A.J. Ludke, and was full of questions.

"First, was my son Billy abused by Father Benedict?"

"I simply don't know," Shane said. "We're piecing together Father Benedict's actions and don't have the whole picture."

"Well, what part of the picture do you have?"

"We know Bella suspected something of that nature. We have an eyewitness report of lewd conduct in a public park by Benedict and another party, an adult, but that's highly sensitive and unproven."

"My God," Sizemore wailed. "Billy hasn't been himself for a year. We thought it was a phase."

"We know certain people wanted Bella to go away," Shane

continued, "and apparently it was about more than airplanes. We know some people have not been forthcoming."

Sizemore said nothing. Shane waited him out.

"But Bella's death was suicide," Sizemore offered.

"No," Captain Sizemore, "we're pretty sure it was murder."

"My God. Who? Benedict?"

"I don't think so. That's why I have to talk to the people who were close to her and especially those who had a conflict with her. You were in her church and she knew your kids. I believe she was trying to protect them."

"A.J. wasn't involved in any of this, was he? He talks big but I can't see him doing anything like that."

"He set off a bomb in her mailbox."

"That was wrong. Stupid. I wasn't comfortable with that."

"But you knew about it."

"He told me."

"Did he tell you he did it for Dot DeGroot?"

This was a stretch. A.J. hadn't said any such thing.

"Dot asked him to put some pressure on her – send a clear message to back off the Growler because the publicity was hurting us with the Pentagon."

"What made you get involved in all this?"

"Fawn and I want to retire here. We always felt it was a good place to raise kids, though now I wonder. I don't want the base closed and my job shipped to Moses Lake or someplace in the wasteland of Central Washington."

"Did Dot approach you to feed her information on Bella?"

"She knew we attended Bella's church and hoped we could influence her to drop the story she was working on. She asked me to talk with Bella and keep her posted. When a county commissioner asks for your help, it's flattering. A lot of Navy guys retire and get second jobs in county or city government."

"So it's nice to have friends in high places?"

"Of course it is."

"Did she say anything about what she would do if Bella didn't back off?"

"Just, 'Don't worry. There is not going to be any article.' You don't think Dot had anything to do with Bella's death, do you?"

"I can't comment on that," Shane said.

"Honestly I feel for the DeGroots," he added.

"How's that?"

"They have a lot riding on Ault Meadows – a lot of unsold homes. If the Navy cuts back on NAS Whidbey, who will buy them? They maintain an upbeat facade, but behind those relaxed smiles, you know they're sweating bullets."

"Understood," Shane said. "For now, I hope I can count on you to treat this conversation as confidential."

Shane punched "end" on his cell phone and returned to his meal.

"Now what?" Brad asked.

"We go with what we've got. It may not be enough, but it's time to sit down with Dot."

Chapter 47

A Good Cigar

"That's a pretty nice cigar. Cuban, isn't it?" Shane asked as he entered the room and sat down.

"Kennedy's favorite," Dot replied as she leaned back in her chair. "H. Upman Petits. I'll give him one thing – he knew cigars."

"You must catch some double-takes," Shane joked. "Not too many women smoke cigars."

"Oh I just play with them," Dot said. "I try not to shock people who don't know me." The county offices, she explained, are a non-smoking campus but she could still savor her cigar. "I just can't light it," she shrugged. "They do last longer this way."

Both of them laughed.

"What can I do for you, Shane?" Dot asked.

"I'm still trying to make sense of this whole Bella Morelli business," Shane said. It bothered him that he called it "business" now, as if his friend's murder were a mere transaction or chore to be done.

"That's what I understand. But isn't it clearing up? We now know Father Benedict murdered her and atoned with his own life, so it seems pretty well settled."

"His suicide note hasn't been released," Shane pointed out.

"The sheriff filled me in."

"And I'm not sure it's authentic. Not sure Benedict murdered her. Not even sure Benedict went over the railing by his own choice."

"Why not?"

"Well, as far as Benedict is concerned as Bella's murderer, we can't place him at North Beach at the time Bella was there," Shane said.

"I'm not sure there is any way to know whether someone went there or not, unless they checked in with the ranger at the entrance station," Dot said.

"Well that's the interesting part," Shane said. "It turns out there is a way. We live in the age of mini-cams."

DeGroot's face reddened.

"But I wanted to ask, did you know Bella very well?"

"Only just a little," Dot replied. "Some friend of hers, Brad somebody, asked me that the other day and I really had to rack my memory."

"You must have had heartburn with her," Shane said, "over the Navy."

"We weren't on the same side of that."

"It's funny she didn't make more of an impression because she left extensive notes in her computer about two meetings with you – one here and one at the offsite field – to talk about the Growlers."

"I meet so many people in this job. The senior moments come more and more."

"And I understand you arranged for some letters in the newspaper discrediting her."

"What are you driving at?"

"I'm just corroborating what we know," Shane said. "Bella's mailbox was blown up by a pretty big bomb placed there by Mr. A.J. Ludke, who says you wanted a warning sent to her about the Growler."

"Good lord," Dot replied. "If he said that, it is absolutely not true. He has a rich imagination if he thinks that's what I meant for him to do. But listen, you and I both know a lot is at stake for this island if bad publicity gets back to the Pentagon. I can't blame Mr. Ludke for being upset.

"Life as we know it will be over. That's a very serious matter, so if you're asking whether I cared about what she was doing, you're damn right I did. I hope you care, too. If we lose the Navy, we're going to have a lot more people jumping from that bridge than just Ms. Morelli."

"I'm trying to make sense of some other things, too," Shane said. "Our department received a complaint of lewd conduct at Goose Rock a week ago – two men engaging in public sex. The witness says he recognized them both, Father Benedict and, I'm sorry to say, your husband."

"That is outrageous!" DeGroot said. "It's without any basis. Whoever said such a thing is engaging in character assassination against a public servant and also a man of the cloth."

"Well I know Father Benedict was at the park at that time because I have his car on video," Shane said. "That's a pretty strong coincidence."

"And do you have my husband's? No sir, I am sure you *don't*."

"No."

"But I do have the two of you on video entering the park seven minutes behind Bella on the night she disappeared."

DeGroot's jaw hung open.

"It's a big park," she said. "We go there sometimes for a few minutes of peace to talk about our day and smoke a cigar while watching Navy jets land and take off around sunset."

"Well here's a coincidence," Shane continued. "Those cigars of yours are quite special – H. Upman Petits. What are they, $15 apiece? Not many people have them with the embargo."

"There's always a way if you want something badly enough."

"So what are the odds that I would find an H. Upman foil wrapper by the log where Bella was sitting at North Beach the night she disappeared?" Shane held up the cigar wrapper Brad picked up on the beach.

"Son of a gun. That's a needle in a haystack," DeGroot said with a big smile. "Interesting but I'm not sure it proves anything."

"Well. Bella never left the park that night, but you left about half-an-hour after you arrived," Shane said. "That's about enough time to walk from North Beach up to the bridge and back. I'm wondering what you did at the park that night."

DeGroot twisted her mouth in a pained expression.

"Well dammit, Shane. Damn, damn, dammit. You got me. I was hoping you weren't going to chew this to the bone," DeGroot said. "I've tried like crazy to distance myself from this whole Bella Morelli business, but you just won't let it go."

There was that word again – business. Shane said nothing.

"Yes, we saw Bella that night," DeGroot confessed. "She was standing all alone by a log at North Beach and it didn't feel right. I felt she was distraught. In fact she was crying. I recognized her and called out, thinking to comfort her. I guess she spooked – maybe thought we were following her or something. She took off with a flashlight up the trail toward the bridge and we followed, trying to talk to her. The more I called out to her, the faster she went.

"Yes, we had our differences," she continued, "but Jeeesus we are not criminals. I wanted to help. She walked out on the bridge. There was no one around. I called to her. She put one leg over the railing and then the other, never hesitated, never stopped. Just like that, she was gone. I never even heard the splash and could barely make out where she hit."

"Why would she do a thing like that?" Shane asked. "What sense does it make?"

"Well I think Bella got herself into quite a pickle and must have been distraught about it," Dot said. "She was the foremost spokesperson of the anti-Navy crowd. I suspect she realized she was on the wrong side of a contentious issue and was feeling great remorse about it."

"So why in the world didn't you report what you saw that night? If it was an outright, simple suicide, why pretend you were nowhere around?"

"Well think about it," DeGroot said. "How would that look? First there's the coincidence of Ms. Morelli and us being at the park at the same time, in the evening. People knew we were on opposite sides of the Growler question. What are the odds people would accept our version and say, 'Oh, what a coincidence. You tried to save her – almost succeeded.' No, this would tie us to her death. They'd say something is fishy as hell about this."

"It is fishy."

"I'm sorry you think that, Shane. Appearances matter when you're in politics. You've gone to a lot of work to imagine something that never happened."

They sat in silence.

"How did things ever escalate like this?" Shane asked. "A lovely woman with cancer moves to Whidbey Island and falls in love with it. She's a bird-lover, for crying out loud. She gets concerned about jet airplane noise and tries to start a conversation about it, and ends up dead because of it."

"Well I think a couple of things are in play there," Dot said. "She uncovered some uncomfortable secrets. People don't like that. And what she was going to write could have devastated the local economy. Do you think Bill Blanchett wants to run for reelection as the senator who lost NAS Whidbey? What would happen to Congressman Brady? Or Commander Fallon? Or Governor Johnson? Or me? Or you? We'd all be sitting ducks."

She continued, "Shane, none of us are perfect. Neither was Benedict and I hazard neither are you. How's your marriage these days? I didn't do anything to Bella. And about that other business, what somebody said they saw on Goose Rock, my husband has a few demons of his own, but he's a public-spirited servant. We do the best we can for the people and that's a fact."

"Damn it, I'm lighting this thing," DeGroot said, reaching for her lighter. "Just a couple of puffs."

Chapter 48

Shades of Gray

"Come on, girl," Brad said, gesturing to Ida. "This is your special spot up front here, where we can mess with each other while we drive. We're going on a road trip. You're going to love your new home in the mountains, and I think Bear is still young enough for a girlfriend."

The big dog jumped up, turned a complete circle, then settled with her nose facing the spot where Brad would sit. Brad turned to Shane. "I thought we had them," he said, shaking his head.

"We had them and they know it," Shane replied. "They know we know, but we can't prove it in court just yet, so the DeGroots win this round. They took an enormous personal risk to silence Bella."

"What happens to you now," Brad asked. "To your job?"

"Well I didn't charge them with anything. On the other hand, I've probably worn out my welcome in Island County. My boss isn't too pleased with me."

"The supreme irony," Brad replied, "is that they went to great lengths to stop Bella and think that they did. But they're sorely mistaken."

"How do you figure that?" Shane asked.

"I have a surprise for them but need some time to work it out," Brad said. "I'll keep you posted."

The two shook hands. Brad opened the door, sat down, gave Ida a pat on the head, and turned the key in the ignition.

When a friend dies before she can write the biggest story of her life, what do you do? Brad asked himself. Do you walk away and say, "What a shame? Somebody got away with something and that's just how it is in the real world?" Life is messy and ambiguous. Tidy endings only happen in stories. Powerful people bend the rules. Truth is subjective.

Brad had ducked the tough stories all his life to write the easy ones, the heartwarming ones, and readers loved him for it. People would rather read the feel-good stuff anyway, the stories that don't challenge them to make hard choices.

His brother's last words still rang in his ears, "Tell the truth, little 'bro."

Wasn't that why he and Bella, and Stu, had gone into journalism anyway, back in the era of Watergate and Nixon and, "I am not a crook?" It seemed a lifetime ago now. The world had changed, or maybe not changed. It was still full of crooks.

Brad pulled out of the Captain Whidbey parking lot onto Madrona Way, past the head of Penn Cove, which was bathed in the gold of sunrise. Great-blue Herons stood like statues in the shallows. The Cascade Mountains filled the eastern horizon. It would be a beautiful day on the road – a day to drive, and think, and take forest walks with Ida. He would not turn on the radio. He needed the silence.

So much of life is gray, Brad thought – not black or white. He'd been so focused on Bella he hadn't thought much about himself till this moment. Stu was dead. Could Brad have stopped him? Bella was gone from his life. He'd waited too long to help her, and now failed to bring her justice. Irene was all but gone. Was there still time to make that right, to make any of it right?

We search for love and get it wrong, and do the best we can, he thought. We devote our lives to something we believe is true and maybe it is, or maybe not. We believe so strongly we break the rules because the pain of losing is simply unbearable.

Was Benedict a bad man – the perpetrator of abuse – or the victim? Or both? People are complicated and contradictory – of that Brad was sure. All have their secrets, parts of themselves that are noble, parts that fall short. Benedict had been a friend to Bella when she needed one. But in the end, had he betrayed her?

And what of Dot and Dutch? Were they corrupt and evil? They alone knew exactly what happened on the bridge that night. The truth wasn't the version Dot was telling, Brad was sure. But was it the version Brad and Shane had constructed in their minds?

At heart Dot seemed a skilled servant. Brad could well understand her long run in office. People liked her. Dot's own economic interests and the county's were inseparable. Is that a bad thing? She was a gracious person, courteous, a good and welcoming listener. What more could one ask?

Would the next person in Dot's office be better or worse?

Ultimately, money and power drive everything. The battle over Navy jets was not about patriotism or terrorism or supporting the troops. It was about jobs and power – governors, senators, mayors, commissioners, school teachers, and corporate America. How can one woman go up against that? Does truth stand a chance against that?

He wondered what would happen to Whidbey Island if it lost the Navy's Growlers, or the base altogether. The economy would crash, he thought, much as Dot DeGroot predicted. But then what? Into this vacuum new and creative enterprises would flow – perhaps a regional airport for air freight and manufacturing supported by the island's educated and skilled labor force. Perhaps a new outpost of Silicon Valley. Perhaps a reinvigorated tourist industry and new outdoor recreation activities. Perhaps in time a groundswell of home building and home sales as property values rebounded from the negative impact of Navy jet noise.

Brad reached the North Cascades alps by midday. He had chosen the northern route for its rugged scenery, good places to take breaks with Ida, and for a last look at Lake Chelan, where Stu's remains now rested. After he reached the old West town of Winthrop he would swing south through Twisp to the town of Chelan. It was the best he could do to honor the memory of a lifetime friend. The scenic drive allowed him time to think.

Bella had fled to Whidbey Island to escape a dangerous husband, and to recuperate from the cancer that had nearly killed her. The island had awakened a new part of her soul, transformed her into someone who found joy in nature and everyday beauty. In every sense she'd undergone a rebirth as she began her second life. She had become the person Brad always dreamed she might be for the life they never had together.

But along with the rebirth, she'd uncovered an existential threat to this wholesome new world from forces with enormous economic and political power.

Dot DeGroot had played her cards well, Brad thought, except for the one card that wasn't in her hand.

Chapter 49

Deception

Brad Haraldsen looked up from his desk at the panorama of snowcapped peaks of Idaho's Sawtooth Mountains. The first rays of sunrise were bathing the snowy crags in pink and gold. It would be another beautiful day, if a bit chilly, and he tucked his stocking feet under the warm side of Ida, curled at his feet.

"She likes that spot," Irene said, nodding toward Ida.

"She doesn't let me out of her sight," he replied. "But I wouldn't, either, if I were her. She's had a pretty big loss."

"As have you," Irene said. "Not just Bella but Stu as well. Coffee?" she asked.

He nodded.

Irene crossed the kitchen to the coffeemaker and poured two mugs. She delivered them to Brad's desk, then sat in the chair next to him and smiled. "You've been up for hours. How's it going?"

"I'm on a roll," he said. "I really think this is my best work ever, the most important."

"It's nice to see you this inspired," Irene said.

"I'm glad to be back home where I belong," Brad said. "Thank you for being so patient and understanding about all this, and welcoming.

I have a lot of work to do here to make things better for us."

"We'll work on that together. Amy and Stu would like that."

"I had the whole drive back from Whidbey Island to think about how much you mean to me, and our home. We have some healing to do."

"We do," Irene agreed, sipping her coffee.

"In a way I didn't foresee, opening our home to Ida is part of that," Brad said. "She's hurting. We can give her the love she needs. You lost Amy a few years ago, and I lost Bella and Stu. There's just us now to care for each other. Maybe that makes it simpler, less complicated.

He continued, "On the drive I thought a lot about what happened on Whidbey Island and the slick way Dot silenced Bella and covered it all up. She thinks it's all behind her now, but there's one thing she failed to understand. Silencing the messenger just makes the story bigger. "

Brad turned back to his computer and the words he was typing:

*

Journalist's Final Investigation Rocks Military Industrial Complex, and Ends in Suspicious Death

By BRAD HARALDSEN, with Bella Morelli and Stu Wood

Special to the Washington Post

This is a story of power, greed, lies and deception. My colleague, Bella Morelli, never finished it but did the hard work before she disappeared off a bridge in the dead of night. Our friend and colleague Stu Wood helped write it before he ended his own life in the dark waters of Lake Chelan, Washington.

This is the story of powerful people who would stop at nothing to keep this story out of *The Washington Post*. It is also the story of three friends who could not accept that, and who stood by each other in death, how ever imperfectly in life.

Deception is the act of making someone believe something that is not true. Our colleague's death has been presented to the public as an act of suicide, the result of depression. We believe the truth is exactly the opposite – that she was at the peak of her career, writing the most important story of her life. The controversy surrounding her death also includes a show of convenient self-deception, the myth that the Navy jet-noise controversy is about patriotism.

In the end, no one can prove conclusively what happened on Deception Pass Bridge the night Bella Morelli fell to her death. Readers can weigh the evidence and reach their own conclusions. In the story that follows, you'll see why influential people wanted Bella stopped, and why the stakes were so high that she paid with her life. *(Continues . . .)*

DAN PEDERSEN

About the Author

Dan Pedersen is a native of Western Washington. He received two journalism degrees from the University of Washington in the turbulent 1960s and 70s, served in the US Air Force and went on to become a reporter and editor for several newspapers in Idaho and Washington, including a large outdoor weekly.

He is the author of six mysteries, many short stories and a weekly blog about nature and small-town life, Dan's Blog.